TRUE LOVE

A Novel By

Destin Bays

"Some love lasts a lifetime. True love lasts forever."

~ Unknown ~

Table of Contents

ENCOUNTER

*"I am like a falling star who has finally
found her place next to another in a
lovely constellation, where we will
sparkle in the heavens forever."*

~ Amy Tan ~

It was early spring, 326 BC, in the beautiful city of Chersonesus protected by a haunting deep blue sea and a giant wall. Today was the second day of the Festival of Dionysus. The local theater presented many plays to the citizens of Chersonesus at the expense of the Greek government. For some, it is this brief period of enlightenment each year that satisfies their thrust for knowledge and the arts.

Today's presentations would start with a tragedy from the great poet Euripides.

Everyone in the city was dressed in their finest, and most were already at the outdoor theater enjoying wine and conversation with old and new friends.

Mikolas had been taking his time making his way from the harbor through the narrow streets to the theater. The whitewashed walls of the homes along the way magnified the bright sun's rays and somehow made the blue sky even brighter. As he walked and enjoyed the clarity of his day, the sound of young women interrupted his thoughts. He turned to see three ladies round the corner in a hurry.

The young woman in the middle was the fairest of the three, and as they passed him she returned his smile.

Mikolas was still mesmerized with the image of the young lady's face, her fair hair and her eyes as blue as today's morning sky.

He was unable to move or change the image of her beauty passing before his mind's eye until the chaperone for the three passed huffing and puffing with a disappointed look on her face. It had been three years since he left his family in Athens to come here and develop a branch of his father's business, and this was the first time he felt excited to be in Chersonesus.

By the time Mikolas got to the theater, it was full.

He stood behind the center of the back row looking for a seat somewhere, in any row.

Then he noticed movement right in front of him.

An older man invited him to sit in a space next to him that had not been there when he walked up. Mikolas quickly took advantage of the offer and sat down.

"Thank you for making room for one more admirer of Euripides' work. My name is Mikolas."

"Don't thank me. It was the young lady that insisted we all made room for you, I just extended the invitation."

"Then thank you for the invitation."

The man smiled and turned his attention to the announcer who had appeared on stage. Mikolas felt himself flush from a small sense of embarrassment. He could rebuild a damaged ship or sail to Athens, but he was having a hard time finding the courage to simply look to his left and see who she was and thank her. The play had started and Mikolas was staring at his feet.

He could not bring himself to look directly at the young lady next to him.

She did have attractive feet. Her ankles were nicely shaped .The only portion of her legs he could see were quite pale.

When Mikolas finally focused on her face, he realized it was the woman who passed him in the street.

Her lips were fuller than the lady he remembered from minutes ago.

Her eyes were still the bright blue he could not get out of his mind.

He knew he was smiling and once again blushed.

She was smiling and waiting for Mikolas to say something.

He found some courage deep inside himself and whispered,

"My name is Mikolas, and I want to thank you for making room for me."

Her eyes had stayed fixed on his, and he was relaxing with her attention.

"I wanted you to sit next to me. My name is Helena and you are quite welcome."

Helena's chaperone was on the other end of the three young ladies and leaned forward to chastise Helena for speaking to a stranger. Mikolas understood her meaning and restrained himself, at least from speaking to Helena. Mikolas tried to return his attention to the play but could not maintain his focus. His eyes would return to Helena, and when their eyes met, both had large smiles and shyly turned away before the chaperone realized they were in non-verbal contact. Helena had also pressed her leg against his soon after the chaperone's comments and had not removed the slight pressure Mikolas felt against his thigh. When the play had finished, the chaperone instructed the girls to follow her back home.

Mikolas whispered a goodbye, and Helena could not take her eyes off him as they left the theater.

INFATUATION

"We choose those we like; with those we love, we have no say in the matter."

~ Mignon McLaughlin ~

"I love coming back into Chersonesus in the afternoon; the city is lit up by the sun beginning to set. The sound of the water rushing past the hull, and the sky is as blue as Helena's eyes."

"Did I hear a woman's name?"

Mikolas, three of his workers along with a friend had taken a small merchant ship out to test the repairs made by Mikolas' boatyard. The sea trials had gone well, and Carpus, Mikolas' friend, was standing with him on the aft deck as Mikolas guided the small ship toward his dock in the harbor.

"You did hear a woman's name. I met a young woman at the theater, her name is Helena."

Carpus was smiling at the irony.

"The name Kleommas has some meaning to you?

"Yes, it's a common name here."

"She has a light complexion, very light hair, deep blue eyes and thick lips?"

"Yes, you have described Helena. Do you know her?"

"I know of her family, as you do. She is Kleommas' illegitimate daughter. The child he loves the most next to his son."

"My largest customer?"

"Yes."

They both enjoyed the balance of the trip through the harbor in silence admiring the sight of the city and the gentle movement of the ship through the water. Once secured to his dock, Mikolas directed his staff and rejoined Carpus. As they walked down the dock and back toward town, Carpus broke the silence.

"You are infatuated by this woman. I do not remember you ever being this emotional about a lady. Look at you, depressed because she is your best customer's daughter. Comparing her eyes to the sky, describing her smile, her jesters. The feel of her next to you."

"Can you help me formally meet her?"

"No, but I think I know someone who could."

LONGING

*"Heaven is not as high as the desires of
the human heart."*

~ Anonymous ~

Helena had been standing by her window looking out to sea, breathing in the fresh air and admiring the picturesque scene of a small ship sailing into the harbor.

She had not been able to think of anything other than Mikolas for days.

His shy smile.

His beautiful large eyes that let her see straight into his heart.

His warmth.

She could not stop her thoughts of his leg next to hers.

The warmth they generated between them told her everything. This man, Mikolas, could be very passionate.

How was she to be properly introduced to Mikolas so she could see and feel his warmth once again? As the small ship disappeared out of her line of sight, she remembered her luncheon the next day. Most of her friends would be attending; someone would know who he was.

Helena thought she had asked everyone at the luncheon before she saw Lamia. When their eyes met, she knew Mikolas had already found someone to speak for him. Helena and Lamia talked of her husband introducing Mikolas to her father. Arrangements for the meeting had already been made.

FAMILY

"… I suppose that it is not so easy to go home and it takes a bit of time to make a son out of a stranger."

~ Albert Camus ~

"I understand your position, Kleommas, but please let me talk a little about his family."

Carpus had been listening to Kleommas explain in a not so subtle way why "This older man is not suited for my youngest daughter." Kleommas was unaware of the time his youngest daughter had spent talking about Mikolas with his wife after just one brief meeting with the man.

"As I was saying, Mikolas comes from a very wealthy and respected Athenian family. Mikolas' father is the premier boatbuilder in Athens. Mikolas has spent many years working extremely hard to gain his father's respect."

"Are you telling me his father is Diodorus?" Kleommas gestured towards a household slave to leave the courtyard. He had instructed his wife to keep everyone out during the discussion of his daughter's future. Kleommas' courtyard was one of the most beautiful in Chersonesus. Kleommas needed to rethink his position and ask one more key question.

"Why did Diodorus send his son to Chersonesus?"

"He had the greatest faith in Mikolas' ability to expand the family business without direct supervision. Mikolas has done well in such a short time."

Helena had been sitting on the floor with her back to the wall under her window that looked over the courtyard. She could not hear every word, but she was feeling better now that her father understood Mikolas' family had greater wealth than he.

"Your persistence has served you well. Have your wife speak to mine and arrange the first meeting here, in our courtyard. Thank you again for taking the time to tell me about Mikolas, we'll see how Helena and Mikolas progress."

"The pleasure has been mine; your courtyard is as beautiful as the stories. You are as wise as I have been told. Thank you for your time."

Carpus was shown to the door leading to the street by one of the servants. Kleommas entered the house to find his wife and give her the news of his consent.

ANTICIPATION

"… We need the sweet pain of anticipation to tell us we are really alive."

~ Dave Kindred ~

By the next week the women had arranged Helena and Mikolas' formal introduction. They were both standing in the courtyard of Kleommas' spacious home along with Carpus and his wife, Helena's mother, a woman Mikolas recognized as the chaperone, various servants and Kleommas standing in front of the whole household. Carpus began after everyone had greeted one another.

"Kleommas, it is with great pleasure that I introduce you to our friend Mikolas."

Kleommas stepped forward as did Mikolas. Mikolas extended his hand and said, "It is an honor to not only repair the trading fleet of a great businessman, but more so to meet his family."

"Well said, young man, your father must be quite proud of his son. I am sure by the impatience of my daughter we need to move to the formal introduction."

Kleommas and Mikolas smiled at each other as Kleommas called for his daughter.

Helena was at his side in less than a moment, and Mikolas could not take his eyes off her.

Her smile was so enchanting.

"Although I believe the two of you have already informally met, it is my pleasure to introduce my youngest daughter Helena to you, Mikolas." Mikolas redirected his attention to Kleommas acknowledging his comment as well as the introduction. Kleommas invited them all to join him for a glass of wine, and they followed him to a seating area in the courtyard.

During the next few weeks Helena, her chaperone and Mikolas spent hours in the courtyard talking.

Helena was a lover of painting and normally worked on a piece while they talked of shared values, family, supporting one another through the balance of life.

The ever-vigilant chaperone kept them from examining or experimenting with the physical desires that had been present since their first day.

Helena also loved playing with the chaperone.

"How many children would you like?"

Mikolas knew she was teasing the chaperone. He could tell some of her moods now by her facial expressions.

Her current look was quite playful.

Mikolas played along and answered her question.

"Perhaps twelve," Mikolas was smiling at her as he answered.

"Twelve. That is quite a few! Have you thought about what twelve children would do to my body and our life together?"

Mikolas was enjoying the verbal game as much as Helena.

He stood from his seat and went over to Helena.

"I had not given thought to the difficulty of birth with twelve children. I had been focused on the conception."

Helena turned from her painting looking up at Mikolas giggling.

"Helena, you know how improper it is to talk of conception", cried the Chaperone sternly.

"Mikolas, from what I understood of your family, I believe you also know that this type of conversation is meant for another time in your relationship with Helena."

Mikolas withdrew from his position and returned to his seat.

Helena was still smiling, and judging from the visible reaction from her body under her sheer chiton, she had focused on the conception as well.

DESIRE

"The desire of the man is for the woman, but the desire of the woman is for the desire of the man."

~ Madame de Stael ~

Spring had turned into summer.

The two inseparable friends were now allowed to walk together with the chaperone a few paces behind.

Mikolas had come to realize that his drive to keep his father proud of him was being taken over by his desire to have Helena respect and love him.

He was thinking of his own family now.

As they walked, Mikolas shared his thoughts.

"I sent a skytale (it was a piece of leather that you wrote on) to my father as I believe he would want to know of you."

"That sounds very serious." It was difficult to see Helena's face because of her kredemnon, but Mikolas could tell from the tone of her voice she was teasing him.

"It was quite serious. I told him about you and of my intentions toward you." Helena's tone changed to a more serious one as they continued to walk.

"And what did you tell your father?" Helena was looking at Mikolas and not watching where she was going on the crowded street. Mikolas took her arm and guided her around several people before he answered.

"I told him I had met a wonderful woman that wanted to try to have twelve children." His smile betrayed his story, and Helena's voice had become playful again.

"Did you tell him to come meet me soon, or he would never see me when I was not pregnant?"

Mikolas was enjoying his playful conversation, "No, but I did tell him we would be married soon."

Helena's heart stopped for a moment.

Her smile broadened as they continued their walk at a slower pace now through the crowded market.

"Do you not think it may be more important to ask me about marriage before you tell your father?"

Mikolas looked over his shoulder before answering to make sure the chaperone was still a few steps behind. "No, I think it is more important to ask your father."

Helena turned to see the broad smile on his face and then struck him gently on the shoulder. "You are an insensitive man, Mikolas."

They were both laughing as they turned the next corner and heard their chaperone greet an old friend. Mikolas stopped Helena's advance next to the wall of a merchant's shop and looked back around the corner to see the chaperone engaged in conversation with her friend.

Pulling back from the corner and turning, he found himself inches away from Helena.

His senses and adrenalin were racing as she stood silently waiting for him.

He pulled her close and embraced her dissolving into her arms.

Helena's whole body was alive and stimulated by the embrace that Mikolas broke off all too soon for her.

"I'm sorry. I…"

"You should not be sorry we are in love with each other, and have strong desires for…"

"Here you are. Helena, you must stay next to me when I stop. I would not want to tell your mother you were out of sight with Mikolas. We should return home."

Turning her attention to Mikolas, "I'm sure you have plenty of work to do, perhaps you can say goodbye now and we will walk back alone after we finish the household shopping."

Mikolas' and Helena's eyes were fixed on each other the whole time.

Mikolas thought the Chaperone might be correct. The desire was a little overwhelming at the moment.

"Thank you for walking with me. I always enjoy our time together. If you feel you are alright walking together, I will leave you now."

"I also enjoyed our walk today and look forward to many more just like it."

SEDUCTION

"Seduce my mind and you can have my body, find my soul and I'm yours forever."

~ Anonymous ~

Most nights Mikolas slept in his small office where he worked on the cost of ship repairs. He had decided to sleep at the end of his dock on some old sail material.

He liked being under the stars.

He needed to try and think about something other than Helena.

The sky was clear and the stars were quite bright.

They wrapped around him but were little comfort, as each time he closed his eyes he saw the longing in her face just before they kissed and could feel the excitement growing inside him until he opened his eyes again.

Helena was also having problems sleeping.

The love she saw in his face just before he kissed her and the feeling that swept over her body woke her only to begin again each time her eyes closed. The end of summer had come and a few Black Sea nights had been cold the past week.

Helena and Mikolas had been spending as much time together as they could.

The days were still quite warm, and Helena and her chaperone had met Mikolas on the low cliffs above the beach facing the sea.

The day was clear, and you could see the meeting of the dark blue sea and the lighter clear blue sky.

Mikolas was pointing out ships in between bites of food or a drink, telling Helena what type they most likely were.

She was enjoying this time with him, as she knew soon enough it would be too cold to spread a cloth on the bluff and share a meal together. Mikolas' focus on the horizon and the ships was quite intense. Helena had not given the sea too much thought before Mikolas.

She broke into his thoughts.

"I've gained a new respect for the sea and a little jealousy."

Mikolas hesitated a moment and refocused his attention on Helena.

"In the past the sea has always been a calming influence for me. If I faced a difficult task or a difficult time, I could come to the sea and do what we are doing today. The sea will not provide the answer to the issue I may be facing, but it has always provided the environment I needed to think clearly. I believe I now have two places I can find that same peace, that same environment to face difficult issues and make difficult decisions."

"Where is this second place?"

"I believe it will be in your arms."

Helena's eyes filled with tears, and she looked away for a moment. Once she had regained her composure, she looked up to find the same loving face she had seen in the street just before they kissed.

"I suppose I have no reason to be jealous of the sea." Helena was smiling again, and touching Mikolas heart only in a way Helena had been able to.

"No reason."

It was hot in the sun, and Mikolas had been working quite hard all morning. They had a small warship that needed to be relaunched on the tide later in the day. Mikolas wanted to cool off and dry out before he went back to work.

"I feel like cooling off a little."

"Would you like us to move down to the beach?"

"That would be nice. We can talk at the same time I refresh myself."

Mikolas finished his wine while Helena told the chaperone what they wanted to do.

Moving down to the beach was just a short walk. Beaches in Chersonesus were large pebble beaches with larger mostly flat stones closer to the cliffs.

Mikolas found a large flat stone close to the water for him and Helena and a smaller stone some distance away for the chaperone. Once they were seated, Helena asked, "Have you heard back from your father?"

Mikolas was still quite warm and wanted to cool himself off in the water.

"Yes, about a week ago." Mikolas stood, and took a few steps to the water.

Helena loved Mikolas' body.

He was strong, muscular and tan from being outdoors most of the time.

Mikolas waded out far enough to dunk himself under the water. Resurfacing he turned toward the beach smiling and feeling refreshed. Helena could now see every ripple of every muscle through his wet clinging tunic.

"He told me he felt it was almost past time for me to start a family."

Helena saw that Mikolas was a little embarrassed to continue the conversation in a loud enough voice to be heard by her as the other people on the beach could also hear their conversation.

She was a little embarrassed herself as she could not take her eyes off his body and wanted to be closer to him.

Helena stood and went to her chaperone to talk, with her back to Mikolas.

He could not hear the conversation but was pleased to see Helena take the kredemnon, she had been using to keep the sun off her head and face, to girt her sheer chiton above her knees. Once they had finished, Helena made her way toward the water over the stones and pebbles on the beach.

The water was a little cold but refreshing to feel on her feet.

Mikolas watched her struggle a little with her balance and began to move toward her. He was too late, she had slipped on a large stone as she became knee deep in the water. The moment it took Mikolas to get to her she had fallen over slowly and immersed herself up to her neck.

Mikolas reached her outstretched hand and helped her to her feet.

As she came out of the water, he realized just how sheer a wet chiton could be. Helena's pale body was completely exposed to him under the clinging garment.

Mikolas was speechless.

Helena was engrossed with her own admiration of his body.

"Helena, are you all right?" the Chaperone shouted.

"I am fine, just wet and feeling a little clumsy."

Mikolas was trying to keep his eyes focused on the chaperone and not Helena's beautiful pale body.

"I will get the sheet for you to cover yourself," cried out the Chaperone as she said to herself, *"and I can dry Mikolas with my kredemnon."*

"I shall dry in a few moments, and the sun feels good already."

Mikolas noticed Helena was trembling a little, as he was still holding her hand and said, "She will dry much faster in the sun without the sheet; she will be fine here with me."

The chaperone could see the same sight he could and knew what was on his mind.

"If you get cold, I will go get the sheet for you." The chaperone was having memories of her own courtship and the slip on the stones her soon to be husband had taken standing in the water next to her. *"I should be so young and that full of anticipation again."*

"Thank you."

Turning toward Mikolas so he could see her whole body, Helena continued the conversation started on the beach.

"Tell me what your father said."

Mikolas' eyes did not know where to look first. They were feasting on the vision before him. When he met Helena's eyes, he realized she was examining his body in the same way.

"I forgot." They both laughed.

REASSURANCE

"You don't marry someone you can live with, you marry the person who you cannot live without."

~ Author Unknown ~

Helena was sitting on a small cushioned bench in her bedroom.

It was actually quite cold in her room, but she wanted to be alone with her thoughts.

Light snow fell across the window.

She was wearing her heaviest clothing.

She had her oil lamp close to heat her hands and longed for Mikolas to be close to help keep her warm.

She had been closing her eyes with each long stroke of her hair and recapturing images of Mikolas over the past months.

Tomorrow, with her mother she would begin the planning of her spring wedding.

Each new day that passed, since the day her father had given Mikolas permission to ask her to marry, was going by very slowly.

Mikolas had approached her father the day after she had stumbled at the beach.

Poor Mikolas did not know what to do when he pulled her from the water.

She stroked he hair again with her eyes closed wanting to feel his gaze on her once more. She desperately wanted his touch, to feel him, to feel his heart racing.

Time moved so slowly.

Tomorrow would bring them one step closer.

She stroked her hair, again with her eyes closed looking for the feeling of their first kiss and the warmth that had rushed through her body. Where was that feeling?

"Helena."

"Mother, please come in. I wanted to talk to you."

SLEEPLESS

"When we are parted, we each feel the
lack of the other half of ourselves. We
are incomplete like a book in two
volumes of which the first has been
lost."

~Edmond and Jules de Goncourt~

Mikolas knew Helena would be talking about the wedding tomorrow, but he was worried about today.

His business had picked up, in part from Kleommas recommending his boatyard to other traders. He was also busy overseeing the house he was building for them. His father had given the house and its furnishings as a wedding gift. His family, except one brother, would make the voyage from Athens to Chersonesus.

Their new home had been designed to be a little smaller than Kleommas' and the courtyard would not be as grand.

His work kept him busy until he tried to sleep.

Almost as soon as his eyes closed, the image of Helena would appear.

She would be standing in the street next to him waiting to be kissed or just coming out of the water at the beach.

Both images caused many thoughts and feelings to awaken in him.

His feelings for her were far deeper than the physical attraction he felt.

Her values, her view of life's meaning, and her desire to be his partner no matter what life handed them drew him back time and time again.

They had developed a strong friendship and a desire to share their lives with each other.

Mikolas was at peace with his choice of a life partner.

He hoped and felt in his heart she had the same feelings.

He would try once more to sleep in his small office on his narrow bed, wrapped in sailcloth, and try to stay warm without her.

EVERLASTING

*"True love never has a happy ending
because true love never ends."*

~ Author Unknown ~

Mikolas had agreed to deliver a repaired trading ship to its owner's agent in Yalos.

His journey would begin early in the morning.

If everything went well on his short sail, he and his small crew would return by land sometime within a week of his departure.

Helena and he had not been separated since they were introduced. The weather was cold and the sailing would be colder. He needed sleep.

He and his small crew departed Chersonesus as Helena watched from the bluff wrapped in her warmest clothing. She could see the small craft leaving the harbor, but she could not make out the men on the boat facing the cold temperature and the light rain that had started a few hours earlier. She knew it was Mikolas at the rudder, and she could see that the crew was rowing.

28

They had very little wind to speed Mikolas to his destination.

Mikolas saw a figure standing on the bluffs and knew it was Helena.

He would instruct his crew to turn east when the wind allowed and sail as direct as they could to Yalos. Mikolas had arranged for horses to speed the journey home and held on to his images of Helena to keep him company.

The boat was small and little shelter was available.

He had agreed to deliver the craft for an owner who was expanding his costal fleet and did not have a crew to sail it back to her homeport after the repairs had been completed. Mikolas wanted all the owner's work and felt the gesture would attract his attention. His crew had been rowing for several hours before the wind came up and they could turn east. Mikolas stayed at the tiller and let the four men that had propelled the small craft forward rest out of the wind.

Nightfall came quickly, and the wind had increased in velocity. The small vessel was moving quite nicely, but Mikolas was very tired of standing at the tiller all night.

One of his crewmembers woke a few hours before dawn and spelled Mikolas. He instructed the man to wake him at first light, which would allow him to make some sittings and confirm their position. Mikolas fell asleep quickly and began to dream of Helena standing next to him in the water.

He woke to the sound of an unfamiliar voice and one of his crew shaking him and gesturing to him to be quiet.

He was disoriented for a moment before he realized they were being hailed by another ship.

Mikolas focused on the man that had relieved him and saw fear in his eyes.

His other crewmembers were lying down so they could not be seen. Mikolas got to his knees and ask the man on the tiller.

"Sarmatians?"

The answer that came back was only one word.

"Yes."

Mikolas was quick to evaluate the wind direction. He could head the small craft toward the shoreline and beach the boat, perhaps get to safety while the Sarmatians got the boat back into the water and ready to sail.

He ordered his men to prepare themselves to trim the sail when he turned toward the coast and row on his command. Mikolas stood to take over the tiller as the first flight of arrows left the much larger Sarmatian ship.

Two of his four men were killed before the second flight of arrows were in the air.

Mikolas had not turned the small craft before he was struck in the back, and the arrow pierced his heart.

SUFFERING

*I believe that imagination is stronger
than knowledge –
myth is more potent than history –
dreams are more powerful than facts –
hope always triumphs over experience –
laughter is the cure for grief –
love is stronger than death.*

~ Robert Fulghum~

Kleommas walked into his daughter's bedroom.

"Mikolas will not be coming back to Chersonesus. At least not on a ship reentering the harbor. I will need your help writing to his family. We will all tell them how much he will be missed, and you can tell them how much you loved him."

"No, you must be wrong." Helena could barely breathe. "I have dreams of Mikolas coming home, sailing back into the harbor. Dreams… almost every night." Helena was weeping as she denied her father's statements. Kleommas gestured for her to stand. He put his arms around his daughter and tried to absorb all her pain, but he could not.

ELENA

*"The future belongs to those who
believe in the beauty of their dreams."*

~ Eleanor Roosevelt ~

Chersonesus had fallen thousands of years ago as a successful Greek city-state.

The ruins had been unearthed and protected for the people of modern day Sevastopol and any other visitor who cared for history.

One person, who lived in Sevastopol, had a special feeling for the site and its history, almost a connection to its sense of being.

Her name was Elena Andreev, and she was about to wake in her small apartment.

Elena had been hot when she went to bed and opened the inner and outer windows so the warm fresh air could circulate through her apartment.

For late spring it had been unusually warm the night before, and Elena rarely used her air-conditioning.

She loved fresh air and disliked the noise and expense of running the air-conditioning.

Her bedroom was quite small. Just large enough for her double bed and one armoire set back in what was an open closet at one time.

The walls were covered with her own watercolors that she refused to give to the gallery to sell.

All the scenes were her images from the Greek period of Chersonesus.

It was not quite 6:00 am when Elena slowly woke to a gently breeze that had been rustling the sheer window drapes.

She had not fully focused her large green eyes or acknowledged her waking state until she heard the familiar morning sounds of several birds in the tree next to her apartment building.

When a gust of wind came from the Black Sea, she could hear the tree's leaves rustling and feel the breeze blow across her bed.

The bed, like most, was low to the floor, and as she focused her eyes outside she could only see the early morning blue sky and a few billowy clouds.

Elena stretched under her sheet closing her eyes again to recapture the early morning.

She enjoyed the late spring and summer; she could sleep without her clothes under a single sheet in contrast to the closed windows and warm sleepwear of winter.

She opened her eyes after one more stretch and pulled the sheet down admiring her own fit body before she found her sheer summer robe and got up to go to her window.

There were no pedestrians on the sidewalk below her window to disturb her enjoyment of the view of the cliffs and the deep blue of the Black Sea just beyond.

The breeze against her face helped to wake her, and the white blooms covering the tall tree not far from the building only enhanced the peaceful view. Her thoughts turned away from the image and feeling she always had standing at the window to her meeting later in the day with her childhood boyfriend.

Elena decided one more hour in bed and then a few hours of work at the American hotel next to Chersonesus would occupy her time before she would get ready to meet Dimitre.

The hotel owners had hired her for her artistic skills and her knowledge of Chersonesus history. Elena had advised them from the design stage of the hotel all the way through the décor in the public areas as well as the rooms. Her excellent English language skills were called on quite often to bridge the communication issues between management and the local construction company.

Just one more hour was all Elena wanted in front of her open windows.

REUNION

"Absence diminishes small loves and increases great ones, as the wind blows out the candle and fans the bonfire."

~François Duc de La Rochefoucauld ~

Dimitre Ivanchuk was waiting at a table in Elena's favorite summer restaurant when she arrived.

Dimitre stood as she approached.

They hugged for a long moment, and as they did, Elena spoke, "Little Dimitre Ivanchuk. You haven't changed."

"You have never called me that in all the time we've known each other, and I'm pleased to see you as well."

They both sat at the table Dimitre had picked almost an hour ago.

He wanted to be early and make sure they sat at his favorite table away from the others. The restaurant had two seating areas. One small area inside the restaurant, that no one liked to use unless it was raining; the other, was a the large patio area with its own outside bar where they were now seated. Elena began again.

"You look wonderful; life must be treating you well."

He did look good to Elena. He had not gained weight like many others. She had always loved his clear blue eyes and his clear complexion. His hair was a little shorter, more businesslike.

"Real estate must be treating you well."

"The crazy Americans are bidding prices up faster than the Russians. The race is on and the Ukrainians are the benefactors."

"Aren't we losing our land either way?"

"We are, but the city is benefiting from higher real estate taxes. It's going back into repairing infrastructure. But enough of my work, how is the hotel coming?"

"The first sections will be open in a few weeks. We should have a grand opening before they start on the bungalows on the bluffs."

"Will I get an invitation?"

Elena was taking some time to answer, adding to the moment's drama for Dimitre. She looked at him against the backdrop of the vines that surrounded the restaurant's patio. He was still a handsome man. His silk pants were a little too shiny as was his silk shirt. Not the best choice for a warm night. He still lacked a little taste.

"That depends on how you treat me tonight."

The real estate firm, Dimitre worked for, had put the hotel deal together and was sure to receive plenty of invitations, but Elena was enjoying the conversation.

"Then we will order the best wine and most expensive meals."

Once they had finished their discussion of the hotel project, they moved quickly back to a time in their lives they were both comfortable with.

The meal came and interrupted a familiar examining look from Dimitre.

He had loved Elena's big green eyes almost as much as kissing her full lips.

The smile was still ever present, and she still made him feel quite comfortable.

Her body had filled out a little in college, and Dimitre felt it had improved her appearance; he had thought her ballerina look was a little severe.

Elena remembered his way of examining her, and after a glass and a half of wine she felt flattered.

She had not been with a man since she returned home from Kiev.

"Tell me about the university and Kiev. I lost track of you when you didn't return home after your first year."

Elena wanted to hear about his marriage to one of her friends far more than telling him about her university experiences. They had time; Sevastopol moved slowly; she would hear his story soon enough.

"You knew my mother wanted me to be a great ballerina, and my father loved art, the human expression of nature as he called it. Well, when I arrived at my first dance class, I knew my future was in art and art history. The National University of Arts and Culture gave me the education I needed to work in several museums in Kiev after I graduated. But I loved the galleries. I didn't make much money, but I loved the interaction with the artists."

"What happened to your dance?"

"I took private lessons for my first two years to make mom happy. It kept me fit, I was not going to make her dream come true and dance for the National Ballet. I simply did not have the gift for dance. I loved art and art history. My last job in Kiev was establishing a small private museum that featured Ukrainian impressionists. The entire execution of the concept was my responsibility, and I loved the project."

"Why didn't you stay on as the curator and director?"

"Sevastopol, Chersonesus, the Black Sea, the sea breeze... I'm not sure, but something made me come home and leave a good job and life behind."

"Men?"

"Let me finish dinner, and you can tell me about your wife."

"Then the men in your life?"

"Some."

"When you didn't come home, I ran into Tatyana in the market in city center. I had not found a job for the summer, and Tatyana's nursing school was out for summer break. We spent a lot of time at first talking about you. A few weeks later we went camping with friends. She didn't have a sleeping bag, and you know the rest..."

"I know. Tatyana stopped writing to me that summer."

"You stopped writing to me that summer, and Tatyana and I were married that next Christmas. She wanted children right away, and I wanted to wait until I graduated and had a job. She finished nursing school in two years and began to spend time with our High school friends while I studied and worked. When her friends started having babies, the pressure on me was very heavy. I had no desire to add a child to everything else I was doing. Tatyana was very upset and moved back home just before I finished my last year of college."

"Do you still see her?"

"As in dating?"

"No just around town."

"Once in a while. We don't have the same friends, but we do see each other and say hello."

"Did you love her?"

Dimitre set his glass down and looked straight into Elena's eyes for some time before he answered.

"I don't believe I did." Still looking at Elena, he continued, "Our relationship and marriage was a rebound from losing you. I'm not blaming you, I think it's just a fact of my life. Do you understand?"

Elena was not prepared to hear Dimitre's admission and could not answer or have eye contact right away.

When she had recovered, she began.

"I was under pressure from my mother to dance and under the pressure I put on myself to make my father proud of me and pursue art. Like you, I was unable to meet the demands of a relationship and pay full attention to my education. I think I do understand."

Elena finished her meal.

Dimitre had not forgotten, just not remembered how beautiful Elena was. He didn't remember her hair being quite as short as it was. He did remember her ever-present smile that reflected the gentleness that he had never forgotten. She was still wearing Levi's, tonight with quite a few holes and well faded, along with a skin-tight top. Her top had a leopard running across her breasts that had always been above average in size.

She was beautiful inside and out.

Elena brought him back from his thoughts.

"Take me home, and I'll find you a better glass of wine, one from Inkerman. What do you think?"

"I'll pay the bill."

MEMORIES

*"You've spent your whole life running
and running, trying to catch up with
something that has never been there for
you. And all you've done is go farther
and farther away from the precious love
that's been waiting for you all the time."*

~ Author Unknown ~

Several weeks after the hotel opening the employees were invited to dine and drink in the large dining room.

Elena and Dimitre had been seeing each other but not sleeping with each other.

Elena wanted a date for the function and felt like having company at home again. They met at her apartment and walked along the cliffs to the hotel and the employee celebration. Most everyone knew Dimitre from his work on the project. They sat at a table with people they knew, some since High school.

"Elena, I didn't know you and Dimitre were back together."

"Well, hello to you. I heard you had three babies."

Dimitre squeezed Elena's hand under the table. Elena had not been too sociable since her return, and a lot of people were just curious about what she had been doing.

"I did, and my husband works here now that the hotel is open."

Elena continued to smile at her old friend until another asked Dimitre,

"Have you seen Tatyana?"

"I haven't."

Now it was Elena's turn to squeeze Dimitre's hand.

They were in for an interesting night. Elena had all the fun she wanted by the time they finished dinner. The bar had been open all evening, and she was ready to leave desert and more drinks to the other guests. Dimitre was anxious to leave himself. He had not seen Tatyana, but he knew it was a matter of time. They excused themselves and walked through the gardens of the hotel back to the cliffs and toward her apartment.

A three quarter moon was out spreading plenty of light across the sea, and the walkway along the cliffs.

Dimitre broke the silence as they walked slowly hand in hand.

"Whatever happened to the boy in middle school that took you to the movies?"

"Gavril Shvets."

"You didn't remember his name at dinner."

"Yes I did. I just wasn't interested in telling the story to eight other people who would tell sixteen, understand?

"Yes I do, will you tell me?"

"Gav and I knew each other only for a few weeks. He had carried my books in my backpack from class to class. He had brought me candy from his home. He had walked me home several times and had been a nice young man. You know mom and I had no money, and when he asked me to a movie on a Saturday afternoon, I said yes. We sat almost in the front row. We were way too close and no one was around us. My suspicions were realized when he put his hand on my thigh just as soon as the movie started. I removed his hand only to find it draped over my shoulder a few minutes later trying to fondle my breast."

They were almost to Elena's apartment.

"Are you going to finish?"

"Let's go in first."

Dimitre followed Elena up the three flights of stairs and opened her door for her.

She went to her small kitchen area which was full with the two of them.

Elena kept brushing into Dimitre, opening cupboards, getting tea for herself and a wine glass for Dimitre.

"Dimitre, go sit, I'll bring our drinks."

Dimitre took the few steps to the small sofa and sat.

Elena's watercolors were all over the living room wall.

One large painting in the center of the wall was an open window with the curtains blowing, the Black Sea and a lone sailboat in the distance.

The boat was an ancient Greek ship.

Other paintings of the Greek theater and the beach in front of the old bell monument surrounded the picture.

"I love your water colors. And your impressions of ancient Chersonesus are quite good."

"Thank you. I am so drawn to the site and the history of the Greek time here." Elena had placed a glass in front of Dimitre and sat down next to him.

"Thanks, I want to hear the end of the story of little Gav Shvets."

"I wanted to see a movie, I had only seen one other. I just kept taking his hands off various parts of my body and listened to Gav saying he was sorry just before he did it again. Like to all the boys that just wanted a physical relationship I said goodbye when he took me home and never went out with him again."

"Was I the same way?"

Elena smiled at Dimitre, setting her cup down on the small coffee table.

"Of course not, you were my first lover. Do you remember our first kiss?"

"As if it were yesterday. I still think you were kissing someone else at the Greek theater, but I felt the magic of that kiss and still do to this day."

45

Elena thought his comment about kissing someone else was a little strange but was flattered that his memory of their first kiss was so vivid.

"Do you remember taking me home that night?"

"Yes, and I remember the dinner you made for me, and the fact your mom was in Yalta with friends."

"You mean that she wouldn't be back that night."

Dimitre turned on the sofa to face Elena.

"It was my first night as well."

Elena took his hand and led him into her bedroom.

DIFFERENCES

Little drops of rain
Whisper of the pain
Tears of love
Lost in the days gone by.

~ Robert Plant ~

Dimitre had not seen Elena for some time. She had been busy working with the hotel owners on the bungalows to be built close to the bluffs. When they started to dig the footings for the buildings, they found large pieces of vessels from the Greek period. Construction had been shut down by the hotel's owners, and archeologists from the local area as well as the United States and Russia descended on the site. The find had been in the paper and news traveled quite quickly.

Elena was deeply involved as a translator and an art historian. It was agreed to start an excavation of the site and delay construction for at least six months. Once everything had settled down, she called Dimitre and apologized for not communicating. He understood based on the newspaper reports of the events and asked if she would like to get away for the weekend. Elena responded that if they could go to Vorontsov's Palace in Alupka, walk in the park and look out over the sea, she would love to go away.

The drive to Alupka was beautiful. For most of the way the road had been set back and above the beach. The mountains seemed to come down to the sea and end at cliffs that ranged from a small number of meters to quite high.

One thing never changed as they drove. The Black Sea was its usual deep deep blue.

As with all trips down this road, the tunnel underneath the dragon was coming, and Elena had a wish to make as they passed through. Dimitre saw Elena's eyes close as they entered the tunnel and heard her hands clap as they exited the tunnel.

"What did you wish for?"

"I can't tell you, or my wish will not come true."

"Do you believe that?"

"If I believe in the wish, I must believe I can lose it."

Dimitre returned his concentration to the road and his music. They pulled off the highway and followed the streets they both knew to the Palace. Part of Alupka was quite old and the streets were very narrow. The late spring day had been cool which limited the traffic and visitors. They found parking quickly and not far from the Palace. The walk to the grounds entrance was filled with the sounds of a few other people, several birds and the chatter of two squirrels arguing over a nut found on the ground. Once inside, Elena headed directly toward the four Lions decorating each side of the wide stairway descending from the elegant rear entrance of the Palace.

Dimitre started the conversation as they stood at the top of the stairs and absorbed the sweeping view of the expansive gardens and the Black Sea in the background.

"I know what I want from life. It's not much different from anyone. I want my life to be richer in experiences than my father's. I want it to be filled with times like we shared that summer night so long ago. I want my own family, but I'm not sure I want to stay in the Crimea."

They had walked down the steps and followed one of the paths that led down to the sea.

The landscaping on the Palace gardens was impressive in the late spring. An abundance of flowers in every color growing alongside, the deep greens of the shrubbery and the trees was enough for any set of eyes.

Placing all of this next to the backdrop of the clear blue sky and the dark blue sea moved the visual experience from quite pleasant to spectacular.

Elena was enjoying the splendor of nature's beauty in a way her father had taught her as she considered her words.

They continued quietly for quite some time before Elena spoke.

"I'm not sure what I want, but I don't want more old boyfriends. I want a man that thinks about me when he is at work and calls to say hello. I want a man that wakes up earlier than I do so he can watch me sleep. I want a man that places his hand gently on my stomach and wonders what it would feel like when I am pregnant with our first child. I want a man that will do what he needs to do to take care of his family. I will give that man every ounce of love and support I have to give. I will never measure him against another man. I will never want what other people have. I will simply enjoy every minute we have together." Elena never looked at Dimitre as she talked. She kept herself focused on the beauty of nature surrounding them and continued as they walked.

"I have been drawn back to Sevastopol, to Chersonesus for reasons I cannot put into words. I will not leave until I understand why I have been brought to Chersonesus."

Dimitre wasn't sure he understood her other than the love of another person was far more important than how much they brought home. He also understood she was not ready to leave her childhood city. The day was cool and Elena had changed their direction of travel onto a path that would take them past expanses of grass and bursts of color from the groupings of flowers in full bloom that occupied the beds designed years ago. When they reached the steps protected by the sculpture of the sleeping lion and his other vigil friends, Elena spoke again.

"Thank you for bringing me here. I'm sorry I've been so quiet. My father loved this place in the spring, and his memory is the strongest here. I'd like to walk the north side of the estate if you're not too bored."

Dimitre was a step ahead and turned to Elena.

"I like the waterfall and the lake. Maybe we can stop at the herb vendor and I'll get some tea for my mom?"

Elena turned on the steps one last time to take in the expanse of the gardens that seemed to spread out in front of her to meet the sea before they walked around the east side of the Palace and up the hill. Elena tried to maintain small talk about school and the people they grew up with, but her mind would wander back to when her father was alive. Each new flowering plant she passed made the image of her sitting quietly on her father's lap listening to the birds in the trees that surrounded their apartment.

From the apartment's small balcony they would sit quietly, observing nature together. Her father would whisper to look here or look there to see a bird or an extra large bloom on a tree or a flower that had not bloomed a few days earlier. She loved this time with her father. When they had been still for just about as long as a nine year old could be, he would ask her to pick out a small piece of nature, a freshly bloomed flower, a bird, a blossom, or the neighbor's old yellow cat with one paw hanging over the edge of the bench as it sunned itself. Once she had her picture, her father would set her at the very small table and have her pick one colored pencil and draw a picture of what she had placed in her mind's eye. Her father died in an accident at work that year, and the memory would bring tears to her eyes.

"Elena, are you OK?" Dimitre had stopped their progress along the path leading to the lake.

"I'm OK, it's just memories of my father."

"You want to go?"

"No let's keep walking. It's so beautiful and peaceful here. We can walk to the lake, get some herb tea and leave the grounds at the top of the hill."

"Sounds good."

They paused at the lake and watched the two swans that had called it home for years and continued on to the herb stand before they left the Palace grounds to return home without spending the night in Alupka.

REQUEST

"To accept good advice is but to increase one's own ability"

~ Johann Wolfgang von Goethe ~

"Mom, how are you?"

Elena's mother was not used to receiving calls from her daughter during her workday.

"What's wrong, Elena?"

"I need to see you."

"Yes."

"I want to talk to you about my life."

"Is it Dimitre?"

"I wish it were."

"When would you like to come see me?"

"Saturday, lunch time."

"I'll cancel my trip to Yalta."

"Mom!"

"I'm happy you think I'm smarter now."

"I'll see you Saturday."

"I'll be a good listener."

"I know, bye."

"Goodbye, see you Saturday. I'll make us a special lunch."

"Bye."

Elena's mother hung up the phone and looked at it for a moment. Her daughter was not in the habit of calling and saying "I need to talk to you". Elena, like her father, had always looked inside for help, not outside. It was only Tuesday, and time would not pass quickly.

GUIDANCE

"The best and most beautiful things in the world cannot be seen or even touched - they must be felt with the heart."

~ Helen Keller ~

Elena had not been to the home she grew up in after her father passed away in quite some time. Her mother would come to city center for shopping most weeks and had always stopped to see Elena on the way home.

The small carriage house was just steps from the street.

The entrance to the living unit was behind the fence that butted to the garage. She used her key to pass through the decorative iron gate as the taxi pulled away.

She followed the pebble pathway to the patio and crossed it to the stairs that led to the living area above the garage.

Her mother was at the top of the stairs.

"Your aunt and uncle said to say hello and asked if you would stop by the main house before you go."

Elena had reached the top of the stairs, hugged and kissed her mom before they both entered the familiar living room.

"Would you like some herb tea before lunch?"

"I would love some, mom."

Her mother went to the kitchen leaving Elena to make herself comfortable on the old sofa many young boys had tried to kiss her on, some successfully. The photos, scattered about on the coffee table, and the fireplace mantle had not changed in years. Most dealt with her growing up, recitals, formals and the occasional local trips she and her mom would make. The one, most special to her, was taken not long before her father died: Elena was sitting on his lap, and they were dressed for church.

She sat in silence as she continued to revisit the memories held within the small carriage house.

Some of her early paintings occupied the same places they had originally been hung years ago.

It was very comfortable to be home, and she wanted to share her thoughts and drink herbal tea with her mom.

Her mother reentered the living room with two steaming cups and two linen napkins. She was using the family china. Elena smiled as her mother approached and received a knowing smile back.

"I'm flattered by the china and linen. I don't know that our conversation deserves all this."

"When your child comes home to talk about life, what could be more important?"

A silence took over for a few moments, interrupted only by the sound of a cup coming in contact with its saucer.

Elena had been gathering her thoughts all week, but it was still difficult to begin.

"I'm at a crossroads. I believe I only have one chance to pick the proper direction. I am 29 years old. Most of my friends have been married for some time and have beautiful children. Their lives seem to be full, and I'm still waiting for something, searching for something I cannot describe."

Elena paused for a moment trying to gather her disconnected thoughts in her mind.

Her mom smiled and broke the silence.

"It's called true love. Most people never find it."

"It's more than just loving someone. I could live with Dimitre. He is in love with me; in his own way he is passionate with me. He seems to be respecting our relationship. All the things any woman would be looking for have been given to me by Dimitre."

"It's not enough for you, Elena, I see it in your eyes. You are very much like your father. He was a dreamer, a believer in fate. He knew his daughter would be an artist. He knew you would wait for just the right person. You are your father's daughter."

"Is that bad?"

"No, absolutely not. Some people spend their entire lives searching for something they can't describe and fail. I loved your father deeply as he loved me. We only had each other until you came into our lives. Times were very hard, but we survived on the strength of our relationship. When your father was down, I was next to him lifting him back up. When I was down, he would do the same. The feelings a man and a woman have for each other cannot be fragile. Life isn't fair sometimes, and you must have strength in a relationship to survive the obstacles. Young people have not figured out that it is much easier to face adversity in your life with the support of a spouse. They don't take the time to feel, to sit quietly and listen to their hearts. Sometimes you just can't find an explanation for a feeling or, it may not seem to have a purpose other than simple satisfaction of the sole. Youth needs to slow down with matters of the heart and simply enjoy. I'm sorry, you wanted to talk to me, and here I'm babbling on about your father and me. Please tell me more about your crossroad."

"I need to go back to Kiev and why, I think, I've returned to Sevastopol and Chersonesus. First of all I have never said I was sorry for not pursuing ballet. I know it must have been a disappointment for you."

"It wasn't a disappointment, I just wanted you passionately involved in something that would provide some fulfillment in your life. Your trips to the balcony with your father showed me you would be following another path. A path that has taken you to the enjoyment of art you have today."

"I always thought I disappointed you."

"You have never disappointed me. Your father would have been very proud of you, and I have always been proud of you from the first day I saw you."

Elena put down her empty cup.

"More tea?"

"Please." Elena watched her mother walk back into the kitchen and retrieve the china teapot she had not seen in years. When her mother returned, she began again.

"You know how happy I was at the gallery in Kiev. I had implemented the owner's concept of his gallery with the best of taste and pride in the works displayed. We had become a successful private gallery, and most living artists were lined up to submit a piece to be shown or sold. I came to work one day and began thinking about my own art, Chersonesus, the sea. Not my friends, and as much as I don't want to admit this, you were not one of the primary reasons for me to come back home. I still to this day do not understand why I gave up a bright future to come back here."

"What did your heart tell you?"

"My heart said go home and paint."

'What did your heart tell you?"

Tears were beginning to form in Elena's big green eyes. She could not answer.

"What did your heart tell you?"

"It told me my future was in Chersonesus. It told me I would find the love I was looking for in Chersonesus. Sometimes I think I'm a little crazy."

As the flood of tears ran down her daughter's face, Elena's mother moved closer.

She put her arms around her daughter.

"There is nothing crazy about a dream. There is nothing crazy about pursuing your dreams. You have never dwelled on what others were thinking or measured your life against theirs in the past. You have no need to now. You may not be running a successful art studio or acting as a curator in a museum, but you are selling your own beautiful watercolors and you are helping to save one of our city's greatest treasures. Continue to follow your heart. It has already led to personal success, and it will lead you to true love."

Elena had stopped crying and her mother stood up.

"Come into the kitchen with me. I've made us a delicious lunch and you can tell me why Dimitre's second chance is failing."

"Mother!"

"He's a nice boy, but missing a little class."

NIKOLAS

*"There is no pain equal to that which
two lovers can inflict on one another.
This should be made clear to all who
contemplate such a union..."*

~ Cyril Connolly ~

Weathermen are overpaid in Southern California.
Ninety nine point nine percent of the time the forecast
would be for sun sometime during the day if not all day.

This late spring day Nikolas Sebastian was sitting on
the beach not far from Balboa Pier. He had come to the
beach to simply be near the ocean. He was still having
trouble dealing with his recent divorce, actually not the
divorce but the sense of failure. He was struggling with
the fact that he had married someone with such different
values and view of life. Nikolas had walked out of his
loft apartment on Balboa Island and crossed the harbor
on the ferry less than an hour ago. He just wanted to sit
on the beach and listen to the gulls and the Pacific
Ocean. He was sitting on the sand with his knees pulled
to his chest and his head resting on one shoulder. He had
pulled his baseball cap down so he would not make eye

contact with the mothers and their children that sparsely occupied the beach during the middle of the week. He had too much work to do to be sitting on the beach contemplating issues he would never be able to resolve.

Fallon had come to the beach to have lunch with a friend at a restaurant at the end of the Balboa Pier.

They had said goodbye in the parking lot next to the pier, and Fallon had taken the blouse and the shorts off that covered her bikini.

It wasn't a good day to drive men nuts, but she wanted the fresh air and the sea.

She walked directly from the parking lot to the hard sand and began her walk up the beach.

Fallon was walking slowly and allowing the surf to come up to her ankles.

Rather than thinking about her divorce attorney and what he had told her before lunch, Fallon was recapturing images of past walks on the beach in other thong bikinis and some of the more humorous responses to her body.

Looking at herself as she walked, she knew her firm and perfect figure was still quite appealing.

Her attention was taken away from the surf and her body when she noticed a man sitting on the sand back and above the beach.

He appeared to have street clothes on and looked a little out of place. She continued her walk until she was right in front of him. Fallon could now see he even had his shoes on, and his hat was hiding his eyes.

She decided to wade into the water and let her bikini attract his attention.

The water was cold, and she was chilling quickly with the Pacific Ocean swirling around her knees.

She looked over her shoulder in between breakers to see if the thong bottom was getting a reaction but only saw his cap still shading his eyes.

Fallon was curious, cold and wanted to find out why this man was at the beach. Now with goose bumps all over, she turned from the surf and walked toward the stranger.

"Excuse me, sir, are you alright?"

When Nikolas looked up, all he saw was a very beautiful, perfect body in a bright red skimpy bikini and the woman must have been a little chilled. Nikolas raised his head so he could see her face and have eye contact before he answered.

Her face was as beautiful as her body.

"I'm OK, I guess I look a little strange sitting here fully dressed."

"Well, I was worried you were a little too depressed about something." Fallon noticed his cap and realized it had Breeze sewn into it.

"Are you Nikolas Sebastian?"

"Yes, but how would you know?"

"My husband is an avid sailor. May I sit down?"

Nikolas was happy for the interruption.

He stood and extended his hand, "And you are?"

Fallon took his hand responding, "My name is Fallon Worth, and if my husband and I were speaking, I would call him to tell him that we met."

"The pleasure is mine". Nikolas realized Fallon had nothing but her bikini on, and her hand was very cold. Nikolas reached down and picked up the hooded sweatshirt he had brought in case it was cold.

"You're freezing, please put on my sweatshirt."

Before she could answer, Nikolas had turned away to shake out the sand. He turned back around to offer it to her.

"Thank you, I am quite cold."

Nikolas held the unzipped sweatshirt open and Fallon slipped one arm in; as she turned to slip in the other, Nikolas saw that her bikini bottom was a thong. Fallon had a gorgeous body. She turned around, zipped the sweatshirt to just below her breasts and put the hood over her head. Even the old sweatshirt looked good on her. Fallon motioned to Nikolas to sit down and took his hand as she sat.

"I was much colder than I thought, thank you for the sweatshirt."

"You're welcome. I'm still curious how you recognized me."

"It was easy. Your hat. Breeze did so well; just days after her launch every wannabe ocean racer was talking about Breeze, and your picture was in all the yachting magazines."

"Thank you for remembering."

"You're welcome."

Nikolas realized, when he turned to thank her, that her body was shivering.

"You're still cold?"

"I think I got chilled."

"My house isn't far. If you like, you could shower. I need to get back to work."

"Another winning yacht?"

"We hope so."

"I'll take your offer, I'm very cold. I don't think the short shorts in the car are going to warm me."

"We can take your car across the ferry, and my house isn't far." They stood and Nikolas began to brush the sand off his Levi's.

"Turn around, I'll do that. You can't see." By the tone of her voice Nikolas knew she was extending an honest offer to help, and she was right, he couldn't see. When she had finished a thorough job of removing the sand, she gave him a little pat and said,

"My turn, please." Fallon turned around, bending a little and waited. Nikolas wasn't sure what to do.

"I'm sure it's not the first bottom you brushed off, and the sand is very hard on the leather in my car. Please."

Nikolas obliged, trying to think of her with shorts on, but it didn't work. A few fast strokes on either side and he stopped.

"Come on, finish up."

Nikolas returned to his task with renewed vigor and removed every grain.

"Thanks, my car is in the corner of the parking lot." She gave the keys to Nikolas, and they crossed the ferry and parked in the carport under the stairs that led to his apartment. At first she was confused and was headed to the front of the house.

"You live back here?"

Nikolas had opened the door to the stairway, turned and smiled.

"I'm a tenant; I lease the loft from an older couple that use the front house on the weekends."

He led the way up the steep stairs to the second floor. The landing was oversized and served as a small enclosed patio. Nikolas opened the door to his apartment, and Fallon passed him and went in. She was amazed when she stepped in. The walls and the ceiling were all exposed wood painted a soft almost off white. It was a loft, not one wall inside the whole room. Nikolas stepped past her saying,

"Come in. It is a little unusual, isn't it?"

"Very, especially for Balboa. I like it. It's so cozy."

Three walls were almost filled with paned windows from floor to ceiling with the exception of the fireplace area. Nikolas took Fallon to the back of the loft. The wall that faced the alley had high paned windows that started about eight feet off the floor and went to the peak of the ceiling. Two small rooms were next to a free standing sink. His sleeping area was divided from the rest of the room by a tall screen that wrapped around two sides of the bed. The back wall also had two matching armoires that must have been over eight feet tall. The table by his bed was covered with books.

"I love your house. You're very neat for a guy."

"Thanks. The shower is through the right door and the bathroom is through the left. Would you like a clean sweatshirt?"

"Let's see when I'm out."

Nikolas went back to the front of the loft and woke up his computer. He needed to get his revised line drawings to his new client, Codros Theophilus. He heard the shower turn on and a little scream, then back off.

"Nikolas!"

"Right there"

"I forgot to ask for a towel."

"I'll get one for you."

"Thank you."

Nikolas retrieved a towel from one of the armoires. He knocked on the door and it opened to reveal Fallon's left hand. Nikolas placed the towel in the outstretched ringless hand and went back to his desk. He needed to get his drawings off to his customer. Once the drawings were approved he could bill for the work. He heard the shower go back on and went to work. Fallon was enjoying her hot shower through the three large rainwater showerheads. Nikolas heard Fallon say, "I love your shower." He didn't respond as he was focused on his email to Codros. Once he finished, he still heard the shower and turned his attention back to the emails that had come in when he went to the beach. Engrossed in writing a response to a potential new client, he had not noticed the shower was off. Fallon had come up behind him and placed both her hands on his forehead.

"Do my hands feel warmer?"

Nikolas was a little startled and turned in his chair. She was wrapped in the white towel he had given her which just made her tanned body look all the better. Nikolas must have turned a little red when he realized he had been staring.

"Don't be embarrassed, I like the attention."

"I have a clean terry cloth robe, would you like it?"

"I liked your reaction to the towel, I'll stay in it for a while. I would love a glass of wine."

Nikolas closed his computer and went to the L shaped cabinets that served as a kitchen and a dining area. He opened the wine cooler under the counter.

"What do you like?"

"A full-bodied red."

Nikolas pulled out a good California Cabernet and opened the bottle as Fallon made herself comfortable on one of the barstools across from him. He hadn't noticed that the sun was quite low on the horizon, and the loft was picking up the colors of the sunset that would happen in less than a half-hour.

"Are you hungry?"

"Bachelors never have any food you can eat, I'm fine with the wine and some conversation." She seemed to be quite comfortable, and Nikolas liked that. He handed her a glass half-filled, poured his own glass and came around the kitchen island to sit next to her.

"You work here and live here."

"I do. Most of my work, once the owner and I settle on a design, takes place at someone else's shop or testing facility. We build small and large models of the design and test them in tanks under different conditions and run the design through elaborate testing programs. Changes are made based on the test results, and we start over until we are satisfied, and then construction starts at some yard some place in the world."

"You must travel a lot."

"I do have a lot of miles on most major airlines and my credit cards."

"Why here, on Balboa Island?"

"I rented a place on the peninsula after we moved the first boat, I designed on my own, from the builder to Newport for sea trials. I was living in San Diego at the time, and the owner lived here, in Newport."

"Your wife stayed in San Diego?"

"That was about the time we separated."

"I'm sorry."

"Don't be. I think we did the right thing. What about you?"

"We separated about three months ago."

"Any reconciliation in your future?"

"I don't think so. I caught him on his sailboat with an old friend of mine."

"I'm sorry."

"With what my attorney is going to make him pay, you don't need to be sorry. Could I have a full glass this time?" Fallon held out her goblet and almost lost her towel. She smiled when Nikolas took the glass and went back around the counter to fill it. He needed to turn on lights as the sun had set. He handed Fallon a full glass and poured himself another half.

Fallon asked, "Did you grow up in San Diego?"

Nikolas had taken the few steps needed to reach the light switches and turned on the two that lit the ceiling. Returning to his barstool, he responded, "I grew up here, in Newport Beach. Went to public school and then on to the University of Michigan. What about you?"

"I grew up here as well, went to private schools and USC. Your Mom and Dad still in Newport?"

"Mom is; Dad still travels a lot. He's a professional sailor and crews on ocean racing yachts. The sun's down, are you cold?"

"Not yet and my clothes aren't the warmest. I would like some music."

"Follow me."

Nikolas took her to his computer and sat down on his desk chair as he opened his notebook. Fallon leaned over his shoulder to see what was in his tunes folder. As she pointed at a folder her towel slipped again. She made no attempt to recover her left breast that was now out of the loose towel.

"What's in your "Mood" folder, Mr. Sebastian?"

"Open it and see."

"Can I sit?"

Nikolas smiled and she turned her back, loosened the towel and recovered herself. She sat sideways on Nikolas' lap with one arm around his shoulder.

"I like this album. How do I play it?

"Like this." Nikolas placed his hand on top of hers and moved the mouse until he could click on the first song. The entire loft began to fill with Celtic music. Fallon leaned over, her towel loosened again, and said,

"I bet it sounds much better from your bed."

DIVERSIONS

*"If our condition were truly happy, we
would not seek diversion from it in order
to make ourselves happy"*

~ Blaise Pascal ~

"Hi mom, I wanted to call and tell you I can't go diving tomorrow."

"I'm disappointed. The students will miss meeting you."

"I'm behind on some of the testing and need to visit the model maker. He's causing part of the slowdown."

"I'm sorry, I'll miss you. How are you and Fallon getting along?"

"We do fine in some areas, but I'm not sure if I'm just headed down the same road again."

"You have a great heart, and you need to listen to it instead of some other part of your body."

"Mom… I know the difference."

"Dad call?"

"Two days ago."

"How was he?"

"Tired. He just finished four hours at the wheel, and, based on the background noise, the weather was a little fierce."

"I think, it's time for him to stop."

"We've talked about this. Dad is an ocean racer. Until they stop calling him to crew, he will keep racing. You going to quit scuba?"

"No."

"I got to go."

"Dinner tomorrow?"

"The three of us here."

"You can't cook."

"You can."

"Tomorrow."

"Bye."

Fallon had gone to bed no more than an hour after Nikolas' mother had left. Nikolas was still working on the most recent tank test results, and he wasn't happy with the performance of the keel. He needed to work on the problem and deliver the new design to the model maker in the morning. From the bedroom he heard:

"Your mother is cute. Has she always been a dive instructor?"

"She has." Nikolas delivered his answer without much interest.

"Has your father always been a dentist?"

"He's a sailor, crew for off shore racing." Nikolas was a little irritated; as he had told Fallon, he had work to do before she made the decision to stay.

"I wanted to see if you were listening."

After some time Nikolas answered,

"I am, but I need to finish this redesign tonight."

"I'm lonely."

"Go to sleep. I will see you in the morning."

Fallon spent five days a week keeping in shape and was not at all happy coming in second to work.

"Breakfast, just me, no work."

"Deal."

Nikolas had been up quite late but was satisfied with his work. He woke to the smell of bacon. He pulled on the denim pants he had dropped on the floor the night before, and went to the kitchen area. Fallon smiled and tended the frying pan.

"Good morning."

"Hi, sorry I missed you getting up."

"I feel a little neglected. Coffee?"

"Please."

Fallon covered the frying pan and poured two cups from a fresh pot.

"Thank you. New robe?"

"No. I picked up more clothes at home, his house. Do you like it?"

"What is not to like about sheer silk over a beautiful body first thing in the morning?"

"And I can cook." Fallon finished the bacon.

"Over easy, right?"

"Please."

As she broke the eggs in the hot pan, Nikolas was seeing the natural side of Fallon, and he wished she would let it out more often.

"A friend is having a party this Saturday night. I think it's her husband's birthday. We, that is you and I, have been invited."

The eggs were done, and Fallon slipped them onto a plate she had pulled from the small oven below the counter.

"Breakfast is served, Mr. Sebastian. I forgot juice." She opened the under-counter refrigerator and retrieved two large glasses of orange juice. Fallon joined Nikolas on the other side of the counter and sat down. Her robe was so sheer.

"Tell me about the party."

"It's just a simple birthday party in Crystal Cove."

"Have you seen me dressed up?"

"You have slacks?"

"No."

"You have shoes other than deck shoes?"

"No."

"You have a spring sport coat?"

"All seasons."

"Everyone wants to meet you. You know, you're a legend in Newport sailing circles."

"I'm not old enough to be a legend. I do business with some very wealthy people, and I have never embarrassed any of them in public. I'll wear my newest deck shoes, my best jeans and shirt, and the sport coat looks great. I can't go to the opera, but I'll be OK at a birthday party with your friends.

"I could go to Fashion Island for you."

"If they don't like me because of Levi's and deck shoes, I don't think they will like me in silk and linen. I'm who I am. I design world class racing yachts, and I have no need to change for anyone. Tell me about the people, not what they put on their backs."

Fallon finished her bite before she started.

"It's a lot of people I went to school with. We're like any group. We get together and talk. Update each other on what's new in our lives, and that's where you come in. People really are impressed with your work and want to meet you."

"That's fair. I'm sorry, I have a hard time with people who're more interested in who you know than who you are."

"Some of my friends can get that way. I think you'll have fun."

Fallon finished her breakfast as well. She stood from her stool and went around the kitchen island to do the dishes. Nikolas started to get up. Fallon stopped him before he had set his bare feet on the floor.

"Last night you said breakfast was my time. Dishes are part of breakfast. You can talk to me. I want to know about your wife. I told you why I'm not with my husband."

"What would you like me to tell you?"

"The whole story."

"We met when I worked in San Diego just out of college. Her father commissioned a boat, and I was the lead on the project."

"How did you meet?"

"At the first tank test. She was quite interested in sailing and was a good sailor herself. We became very close during the project and married. I continued to work quite hard, many hours, and we never developed friends or a life together. Her father continued to support her during our marriage."

"That must have been nice."

"In truth, no. She lived beyond our capability with her father's help, which just continued to fuel her unrealistic expectations about our financial future."

"He must have been quite wealthy?"

"He was, and actually quite a gentleman through the whole relationship. Once I opened my eyes, I saw just how different we were. Our values, and view of what's important in life weren't in sync."

"Why divorce? Why not counseling?"

"When she wanted to be pregnant like her friends, I saw her wanting another possession, like a car. "Everybody is having them, we should." That was her favorite closing line to a discussion. She was more interested in where our house was rather than understanding that anywhere we lived was our home as long as we were together. You understand?"

"Most of what you're saying. But you're doing much better now. You have your own business, and your customers are very wealthy."

Nikolas smiled and thanked Fallon for breakfast.

CLARITY

"Clarity of mind means clarity of passion, too; this is why a great and clear mind loves ardently and sees distinctly what it loves."

~ Blaise Pascal ~

"Dad! Where are you?"

"LAX, your mom will be here soon, and I'll be back in Newport Beach in a few hours."

"Will I see you this trip?"

"Tomorrow morning if you like. I want to see your new boat and hear about Fallon."

"Breakfast?"

"I'll see your mom and her group off to Avalon and come over."

"She's diving in the kelp right off Avalon again?"

"With fifteen students and a few other instructors."

"I need to see you. I think my compass could use an adjustment."

"Your compass is fine, you need to tell your brain being alone is OK. I love you, son, see you in the morning."

Nikolas hung up thankful his father was home. His trip to Crystal Cove for the birthday party had been a little depressing.

Nikolas answered the door buzzer with a loud "come in", and his father walked back into his life again as he had done so many times in the past. Nikolas got up from his desk and went to his dad. They hugged for a long time before Nikolas spoke, "I've needed you the past few weeks."

"Let's go to the Galley for breakfast, and then I'll take you sailing."

"I need to talk, I need your advice."

"You can tell me a little at breakfast, and we can talk on the boat."

"I'll take you downtown for breakfast, and we can talk walking around the island. I need you to hear me, and I need your advice."

"It's that serious?"

"It is."

"The Patio Kitchen it is."

Nikolas locked up and met his father in the alley. They walked along the sidewalk between the homes facing Newport harbor and the narrow beach that surrounded the island. They tried to figure out the first time they had walked the bayfront together. Halfway to the restaurant his father asked, "How's the boat coming?"

"I was stuck on the keel for a few weeks, but I seem to be past that."

"What do you think of her?"

"The boat or Fallon?"

"The boat. We can talk about Fallon on our after-breakfast walk." Nikolas shared the reasoning behind his latest design until they got close to the restaurant. They ordered breakfast and his father commented, "The word on the ocean racing circuit is your design for Codros may be another breakthrough."

"I think the rumor mill is a little overactive. Codros and his engineers like the design. I had a lot of problems with the keel. My most recent work changed all that based on our tank tests the past few days. I believe this boat will be one of my best efforts, but breakthrough? I don't know."

"That's good to hear coming from you. When will you start building?"

"I'm a few weeks behind schedule and need to make up the time. Codros, as you know, is a shipbuilder and we've agreed, subject to my approval, that he'll find the yard."

"Anything on the horizon after this project?"

"Lots of inquiries, lots of discussion, but no contracts."

"You always get a new project, and you always create a winner. I think I know what's going on here. Just correct me if I get off course."

They finished breakfast and were just drinking coffee. The restaurant was full and Nikolas was a little uncomfortable.

"I'm going to pay the bill, you grab the bench at the end of Marine. I want to hear what you say in a little more privacy."

"Deal."

It seemed to take forever to pay the bill and rejoin his father at the bay-front.

"Sorry, the service is great until you want to pay."

Nikolas' father smiled and just looked at his son for a few moments before he started again.

"Old sailors tell long stories, so just bear with me. I'll get it all out eventually."

Nikolas returned an understanding smile as his father began.

"Since you were a little boy and I took you sailing for the first time, I knew once you found your course, you would not deviate until you were successful. I'm sure, you remember me coming home and taking you sailing. You wanted to please me, and I just wanted to spend time with my son. You focused on what we were doing and listened to me. In a matter of minutes you would understand what I said and would apply what you had learned. You were probably a better sailor than me by the time you were eleven. As you grew, you demonstrated time and time again how focused and successful you could be when you set your own goals. I was so proud of you. From middle school through high school my favorite employer and friend became your mentor and greatest supporter. He recognized the same things I did. Thank God he decided to invest in your future. All of us have tremendous faith in you. None of us worry about your continued success. Just keep doing the good work you have always done, and the people with enough money to appreciate what you do will find you."

Nikolas broke in, "Then why am I sitting here feeling worried about tomorrow when all the people I care for tell me not to?"

"I'm getting there."

Nikolas and his father smiled at each other as a jogger stopped at the sea wall to stretch before she began her run.

"Your problem is not your business head. For some reason, you have always needed a woman in your life. It started very early, and it continues today. You don't seem to be very objective about your relationships; sometimes I believe you worry about being alone too much.

I'm not telling you to apply cold logic or your slide rule in your personal life. You have good instincts in business, in your work. You just need to listen to what your instincts are telling you in your personal life."

Nikolas acknowledged.

"You remember, you were fourteen years old?"

"Allison Howell."

"Yes, Allison Howell. By the way, her father really was a dick. Your mom told me about that call."

"She dumped me for Keef Landon."

"You hung out with her for a long time, over two years. Her father wanted her to spend more time with a higher class of people. She broke your young heart."

"She did. I wanted to kick Keef's ass."

"You didn't for all the right reasons."

"I know, her dad was a social climbing jerk, and Keef was as innocent as I was. By the way, she dumped him for some wealthier guy she met in college."

"My point in all this was I'm sure you knew Allison and her family had a very shallow view of a person's worth, and yet you stayed with her for a long time."

"As long as we're on the women of my life, what about Ashlee Morgan?"

"You were both in college; you were both focused on your studies; and you were both convenient. You understood what was going on and so did she. The relationship worked, in that it satisfied your need to have a woman in your life"

"You're on a roll. What about Brittany?"

"Your wife was a product of your slide rule. You had graduated from college. You received a job offer most people in your profession only dream about. Your talent was recognized right away, and Brittany was there at the exact time your slide rule told you it was time for you to get married. Your mom saw it; your friends saw it, and I bet you knew it but desired the companionship more than the thought of making a mistake. This is when I feel selfish for spending most of my life on the deck of a sailboat instead of at home with my family. I think it's time to head back to your loft; the rest of this conversation could be overheard."

Nikolas agreed and also needed to check his email. The walk back up the bayfront was quiet, and Nikolas kept thinking about his father's statements. Once they settled into the overstuffed chairs in the loft's living room, his father started from his last comment.

"I want to hear about Fallon."

"Good time to ask. I'm trying to figure out what's going on, and she's the reason I wanted to talk." Nikolas gathered his thoughts before he continued.

"I enjoy spending time with her. She is bright, she is beautiful, but I'm afraid she is a little shallow."

"Another product of her environment?"

"I think so. We went to one of her friend's home for a birthday party. It was a typical young Newport Beach group more interested in who you know and what you have instead of who you are."

"What do you think the problem is?"

"I'm not sure, maybe we just need some more time together to understand each other. She has a natural side she needs to let out more often"

"Have you considered that both of you may be rebounding from the wrong relationships, and you're just not suited for one another? Have you thought, for more than a moment about giving Fallon more time?"

"No, but you may be right. Both of us rebounding and clinging to one another makes more sense than sharing a great deal in common and loving one another."

"Out there, in this world that has become so small, is a young woman waiting for you. She has the same values you do; she is creative like you are, and I hope she will release your heart as your mother did mine. Show me your newest creation."

ADVENTURE

*"All journeys have secret destinations of
which the traveler is unaware."*

~ Martin Buber ~

Recent tank testing and velocity prediction programs pointed to the results Nikolas had been looking for. He sent off a complete package for his client's approval and was waiting for the call scheduled by email. It was almost eight PM in Athens, and Nikolas had only been up for three hours. Fallon had left early to meet a friend for coffee. When his phone rang, Nikolas took in a deep breath before he answered.

"Hello."

"Nikolas, she will be the finest racing yacht ever built. I want to thank you for your best work. She is unbelievable on paper! I cannot wait to start construction."

"You like the design?"

Codros laughed a little and continued the praise, "If my wife finds out how much I love my new boat, she may divorce me."

It was Nikolas' turn to laugh. "I'm glad you like her. Have you named the boat yet?"

"I believe I have, but I want to see her first. I want to talk to you about the metal process that was brought to me for large ships. We might want to consider using it on our new boat."

"What is it?"

"A solution, a treatment that is applied to aluminum. It's supposed to enhance the strength without reducing other properties."

"Do you think it might perform better than today's composites?"

"I'm not sure. I have my engineers working on the information presented to us. I would like you to meet me and the people that have developed the process."

"When and where?"

"That's what I wanted to hear. When is in a few days. Where is Ukraine, the Crimean peninsula, in the city of Sevastopol. Have you been to the Black Sea?"

"No, but it sounds interesting."

"I'll have my travel department call you first thing in the morning about your itinerary. They should call about 10:30 tonight your time. You are going to love Sevastopol and the people. See you in a few days. Thank you for the boat."

"It has been my pleasure, and I know you'll win the Cape Town to Rio Race."

"Thanks again, Nikolas."

FAREWELL

*"If you love somebody, let them go, for
if they return, they were always yours.
And if they don't, they never were."*

~ Khalil Gibran ~

Elena and Dimitre had watched the sun go down, sitting on the bluff above the beach.

The moon was almost full, and its light sparkled like diamonds scattered across the blue velvet of the Black Sea.

Elena sat for some time breathing in the sea air with her eyes closed before she spoke.

"I want to walk the old streets on the way home. Sometimes I feel like I can hear the voices of ancient Chersonesus as I pass through the village."

Dimitre enjoyed the time spent in quiet simply because Elena did.

He did not share her feeling for the ancient site.

They walked back from the cliff toward the arch that had been reconstructed.

Elena sometimes had visions of the homes they would be passing and images of people passing them in the street.

She was always looking for one person, one that was always just a little out of sight.

It only took a few extra minutes to walk through the streets and pass the temple that had been built in honor of Dionysus, the god of wine.

They were on the path headed toward the hotel when Dimitre spoke.

"At times I feel you are searching for someone. I'm not sure, but I believe you may be looking for a man you have not met."

Elena was impressed with Dimitre's perception.

"I believe sometimes I'm doing as you say. The problem for me is I don't understand why."

They continued in silence enjoying the gentle breeze and the sparkling diamonds.

Elena was unconscious of the fact that she was not holding Dimitre's hand.

Dimitre was very aware and worried about the relationship slipping away again.

When they reached her apartment, Elena turned to Dimitre.

"I have no idea why I'm so tired this early. You're welcome to stay, but I'm going to sleep right away."

Elena was awake a little before sunrise.

She could hear the birds' first communications of the day.

She had been looking at Dimitre sleeping until tears began to form in her eyes. Elena could not remove the conversation, she had with her mother, from her mind, and she could not continue her relationship with Dimitre.

It would be unfair to him.

The images that had awakened Elena earlier had come from her dreams many times in her life, but never as intense. Vivid enough to wake her, but still the images of faces were just out of sight, not to be fully recognized.

She left Dimitre to his sound sleep and went into the kitchen and made a cup of herbal tea for herself. She was sitting on the sofa dealing with her thoughts of how to let Dimitre down as gently as possible when her phone rang.

"Yes."

"Elena?"

"Yes."

"It's Yasha."

"I know."

"Are you alright?"

"It's just early, I need to wake."

"I'll call later."

"No. No. I'm fine."

"Day after tomorrow we have a special guest and his friend coming to the hotel. His name is Codros Theophilus."

"The Greek shipbuilder?"

"Yes, and his friend is a racing yacht designer from California. Mr. Theophilus wants a guide to show him and the American through Chersonesus Saturday morning. Depending on the level of interest the American has, it may take all day. I know you love to paint on the weekends, but would you?"

"The American must have a name."

"Yes, yes. One moment. Here, his name is Nikolas Sebastian."

"That sounds Greek."

"He's from California, will you help?"

Elena thought for a moment. It would give her a chance and an excuse to back away from her plans with Dimitre for the weekend.

"Yes, I will be happy to show them Chersonesus, but I don't think Mr. Theophilus needs a guide."

"He would like the American to have a good feeling about Sevastopol and most especially Chersonesus."

"I'll see you later, thanks. It should be fun."

Elena was still curious about a man from California with a Greek name.

She needed to wake Dimitre and cancel their weekend plans.

SEVASTOPOL

*"...perchance, more virtue is being
practiced at Sevastopol than in many
years of peace. It is a pity that we seem
to require a war, from time to time, to
assure us that there is any manhood still
left in man."*
(The Crimean War 1854 - 1856)

~ Henry David Thoreau ~

The sun was just setting as the small commuter jet touched down on Simferopol airport's runway.

Nikolas had traveled twenty-two hours to this point and was happy to be finished with flying. He had cleared customs in Kiev and only needed to claim his bag and find his driver. As he passed through the gate to the front of the small terminal, he saw a young man holding up a sheet of paper with his name on it. Nikolas worked his way through the small crowd of people that had gathered to greet passengers from his flight. Nikolas made eye contact with the man and received a nod as recognition. His driver introduced himself followed by saying how bad his English was. Nikolas just smiled and followed him to his car. He had been told the drive would take a little over an hour, and that he shouldn't worry if the driver did not speak English. Comfortable in the back seat of the small sedan, he watched as they passed through Simferopol, a good-sized city.

When they reached the countryside, Nikolas returned to his thoughts about Fallon.

He was resolved to the fact that he was not in love with Fallon, and at best they were both rebounding from their last marriages.

He concluded he should let her know as soon as possible but had not decided how he could tell her. Maybe now in the dark countryside he could find the solution. He was almost asleep sitting up when he heard the driver.

"Inkerman over river. First Sevastopol." His driver was pointing to what looked, from the lights, to be a small village.

"Hotel not long."

Nikolas was happy for the interruption and was looking forward to seeing Codros and settling into a comfortable bed. When they pulled up the pebble drive to the hotel's entrance, he could see his Greek client waiting with a very large smile.

Nikolas was no more than two steps away from the car when two strong arms were wrapped around him giving him a hug.

"I'm so glad you are here." Codros stepped back and extended his hand.

"Welcome to Chersonesus, a great Greek city-state founded in 421 BC".

He took Nikolas by the arm and walked him through the open entrance to a Greek columned lobby. Instead of guiding him to the front desk, Codros took him to a small lobby bar. When Nikolas looked over his shoulder, he saw his bag handed from the driver to a bellman.

"Don't worry, you're checked in and your bag will be in your room. Please sit. I want to look at you eye to eye and thank you once more for the beautiful yacht." The two men sat at a small table that had already been set up for them. A bottle of wine and a little finger food had been laid out. Codros sampled some of the food, giving Nikolas time to speak.

"Thank you for making all the arrangements. Everything went very well, and this hotel is beautiful."

"It has been my pleasure. I have not been this excited about a project in many years. You have brought a great deal of joy into my life, and I have been waiting to thank you in person. You are a very talented and gentle man; I want to thank you from my heart, and I hope you find the love you seem to be searching for."

"Thank you for your faith in my talent."

Nikolas had only met Codros once before. He had been told he possessed a very keen sense of people, but Nikolas was a little unsettled by his statement.

"You like the wine?"

"It's very good."

"Crimea is known for its wine. They have been growing grapes and turning them into wine here since before Christ. My ancestors worshiped the god of wine here. Inkerman is one of the best wineries in all Crimea."

"The driver pointed into the dark on the way and said, "Inkerman over river.""

Codros smiled, "You will love the people here. Our guide tomorrow speaks perfect English and has an art history education. She has helped the Americans develop this property in the spirit of the old city-state. Eat, Nikolas, eat, drink and then sleep; we will have a wonderful day tomorrow on our personally guided tour of Chersonesus." Codros brought him up to date on the schedule they would keep over the next few days.

The two would spend the day together tomorrow.

Sunday and Monday Nikolas would be on his own as other business in Sevastopol needed his Greek client's attention.

On Tuesday they would meet with the metal treatment people and decide what to do next Tuesday night.

Nikolas thanked him again for the opportunity and picked up a key to his room from the desk. The room was on the third floor, facing the Black Sea. When he opened the door, he could feel the rush of cold air from the air-conditioning. His bag had been set on the caddie next to the armoire. He found the control for the air and shut it off. His room had windows that started a little below waist height and went to the ceiling.

They opened in and the gentle breeze, that entered his room, was wonderful and fresh.

Codros may be right: the Black Sea in front of him and an onshore breeze; what more could he need for a good night's sleep?

DESTINY

*"Two souls and one thought, two hearts
and one pulse."*

~ Helena Ivanovna Roerich ~

Elena and Nikolas were both up at dawn.

By the time Nikolas was dressed and ready to go, he still had two hours before he would meet the guide and Codros in the lobby. His view of the Black Sea was spectacular, and he could just make out some ruins in the near distance when he leaned out and looked to his right. He decided to go to the lobby and see if he could find coffee and take a walk. He felt far too excited for a tour of some ruins. Something was telling him to take a walk; he just wanted to get outside.

Elena could not stay home for two hours, and she had left her apartment and walked to the hotel. Something was moving her, exciting her, and it wasn't simply the thought of spending time with a Greek and American man touring Chersonesus. She was far too excited. She entered the hotel lobby and crossed the space between the open doorway and the front desk, said good morning to the staff and headed for the coffee table discreetly set up by the small lounge. As she passed the elevator lobby, she noticed one of the cars was coming down, quite early for a guest. Elena wanted her green tea and a walk in Chersonesus.

The elevator doors opened a few moments later, and Nikolas stepped out.

He went to the desk to ask about coffee.

The only staff member was answering a call and speaking French when he arrived.

Once finished, the person behind the desk made eye contact with Nikolas and said in perfect English.

"Coffee, sir?"

Nikolas smiled, "Thank you, yes please."

"If you go straight across the lobby past both sets of columns, turn a little left; you will see the table we set up every morning. Coffee, hot water and tea."

"Thank you."

As he cleared the first set of columns, he could see the silhouette of a young woman on the other side of the expansive lobby walking quickly toward the entrance.

Nikolas continued past the second row of pilasters and saw the table to his left, but the young woman had already cleared the front entrance.

He took a paper cup and filled it about halfway with coffee and headed toward the front of the hotel himself.

Once outside, he admired the gardens for a moment and saw a pebble path leading off to the right.

The coffee was strong and the gardens were beautiful with the morning dew still clinging to the plants and blossoms.

With all this beauty surrounding him, he could not get the silhouetted figure out of his mind.

Reaching the edge of the property, he saw a newly placed sign, written in several languages, pointed to another path.

The sign simply said "Chersonesus."

Nikolas felt drawn to follow the path as well as the young lady along the bluff toward the ruins.

The walk felt good. The air was fresh, and a light breeze was coming off the sea. The rock beach below the low cliff was quite different from the sand beaches at home but not unfamiliar, almost haunting with a gentle swell washing over the polished stone. Movement caught his attention.

He could see a very large bell hanging from something on top of a slightly elevated position just past some ruins. He was sure the woman, he had seen at the hotel, was standing between the bell and the bluff, looking out to sea.

Nikolas was getting quite stimulated by his pursuit and quickened his pace. As he passed through a ruin with columns on each side of the structure reminding him of a temple, he felt, he had seen before. He saw the figure ahead of him move away from the bluff toward a small hill and some buildings.

Elena was disappointed to see someone crossing through the Roman Basilica and headed her direction. She had come to Chersonesus to find her emotional center and relax before her day began. She decided to go to the theater. The time she spent there never failed to give her the peace she needed. Today was not going the way it should or had at all times in the past. Something was stimulating her senses in a way she had not experienced before. Looking at her watch as she made her way past the museums and the old Greek mint, she realized she still had a little over an hour before she needed to be in the lobby of the hotel, plenty of time to relax.

Nikolas could not read the engraved metal plate on the large bell's supporting structure but knew he would hear the story of the bell during his tour.

He felt drawn toward the elusive young lady that had disappeared between several low buildings on the hill behind him.

He was quite curious and even exhilarated by the thought of meeting her in a place like this.

He followed the narrow Grecian streets that once led through this side of the ancient city.

He passed under an arch on his way to the same path that took the distant figure between the buildings.

He was not taking his time or pausing to view the ancient relics displayed in the secured structures along the path.

He realized he was far too eager to find the figure he now felt was the same person he had seen in the hotel lobby as well as next to the bell.

Another split in the pathway and before he saw the sign, he knew he needed to go in the direction of a theater.

Elena was sitting almost in the center of the back row looking out over the theater and trying to imagine what it was like to come to a play in 400 BC. Her imagination was not redirecting the feeling of anticipation and now arousal for some unexplained reason.

Nikolas stopped suddenly when he saw the back of a young blonde lady sitting in the back row of the theater just a few meters from him.

He was questioning why he had come to this place, and why the thought of meeting this woman was so intoxicating to him?

PRESENCE

"It is wrong to think that love comes from long companionship and persevering courtship. Love is the offspring of spiritual affinity and unless that affinity is created in a moment, it will not be created for years or even generations."

~ Khalil Gibran ~

Elena sensed a presence behind her and felt no fear. When she turned and saw the man standing before her, she understood the feelings she had been running from since she had prepared her tea in the hotel's lobby. When their eyes met, she felt she had known him for a very long time. His smile was familiar in some way as was his examination of her. She did not know how long the two of them could keep smiling at each other and not say hello.

"You must be Nikolas Sebastian."

Now Nikolas was really confused, and it must have shown on his face.

"I'm your guide for the day, Elena Andreev. It was your baseball cap, silk shirt and cargo shorts that told me you were an American. Please join me. It is quite peaceful here in the morning. Sometimes I can almost sense the ancient actors. Please sit, we have a little time."

"Thank you."

Nikolas felt no embarrassment or apprehension. He sat next to a beautiful young woman he had met only a moment ago like he had known her his entire life.

"Do you like our beautiful city?

"Chersonesus?"

"Yes."

"I have never been here in my life, but I feel as if it should be familiar to me. Does that make sense?

"Yes. Chersonesus had a similar effect on me when I first came here."

Nikolas was still searching Elena's face for someone he knew.

No one had such large green eyes.

No one he knew had such a sweet smile.

Elena's smile broadened knowing Nikolas was so enchanted by her.

"I come here to think when I have turning points in my life."

"I hope I didn't interrupt your thoughts."

"You have not." Elena's smile broadened again.

"Were you the elusive figure in the hotel lobby earlier?"

"Getting tea?"

"Yes."

"I believe, I was. You must have been the approaching figure when I was focused out to sea."

"I was. I wanted to know who was up this early, and I must admit, I had quite a sense of excitement take over when you walked away from the bluff."

"That's interesting, as I was trying to rid myself of the excitement I was feeling."

They were both pleased at how easy it was to talk to one another. Their eyes did not leave each other for more than a moment, however Elena was aware of the time.

"You should walk me back to the hotel and introduce me to Mr. Theophilus."

Nikolas stood offering his hand for assistance. Elena accepted his offer and their hands touched for the first time. Nikolas felt an immediate and pleasurable stimulation from the simple touch of their hands. Elena was a little startled by her body's reaction to his touch, but she didn't let go of his hand until they were well on their way back to the hotel.

"I thought we would start our tour at the entrance to the city and end the tour where we met. Have you read anything about the city-state of Chersonesus?"

"I haven't. The time between Codros asking me to come and my departure was very short."

Nikolas was so involved in continuing his eye contact with Elena, he was not watching where he was going. Elena took his arm, while he was speaking, to guide him away from some of the obstacles between the theater and the path back to the hotel.

Nikolas was well aware of Elena's body next to his as they walked.

He was hoping a light conversation would take his mind off the physical attraction and contact.

"You grew up in Sevastopol?"

"A small community, that is part of Sevastopol, called Inkerman."

"I saw it last night on the way to the hotel from the airport."

Elena gently guided him away from the edge of the bluff just before they reentered the hotel gardens. She was so flattered by his attention and his reaction to her touch. They reached the driveway and walked toward the entrance, focused on each other and their conversation.

"Excuse me. Excuse me! Are the two of you looking for an older Greek man in need of a guide and a yacht designer?"

Nikolas' face flushed as they turned around to see Codros standing at the edge of the driveway with a very large smile.

Elena introduced herself and apologized. "I guess Nikolas and I were lost in our conversation, I'm so sorry."

"No apology. Sevastopol is much closer to Athens than Balboa Island. If Nikolas likes the people here, he'll come back."

"I love the people here, and perhaps I won't leave." Codros looked at their guide for a response. He saw a blushing face and her hand requesting Cordros' arm. She led both men back down the path toward Chersonesus without responding. Elena spent the balance of the morning telling her two captivated men the story of the establishment of Chersonesus by the Greeks, walking them through the fortifications, the killing field and the military barracks next to the entrance to the city.

She finished her explanation of the military's role in protecting the city from frequent attacks by the Scythians and then by the even more warlike Sarmatians. As they stood in the middle of the military housing, Nikolas was redirecting his attention to the bay just behind the barracks area when Elena would pause her talk about the site's history. Elena could not help but notice Nikolas' interest in the harbor.

"Let's move on to the harbor; Nikolas appears to have a special interest in the harbor's history."

The three of them walked over the small rise behind the barracks and toward the water. Nikolas was walking ahead of Elena and Codros. He was confused and excited at the same time. Nikolas removed his deck shoes and waded into water about half way to his knees, turned and faced the shore. Codros and Elena stood next to the water watching him, waiting for him to explain.

"The feelings I'm having are like coming home after being away for a long time. This isn't my home, and I'm a little confused. I must sound a little crazy."

Elena reassured Nikolas. "Many times during one of my tours someone will feel as if they know the place or have been here in the past. I had a very nice American leave St. Vladimir's Cathedral. He had a brother die before his time, and the American had gone in to light a candle for him. After he lit the candle, he became very emotional and could not stop sobbing. He left the cathedral and was still overcome with grief until he moved fifty or sixty meters away from the church. I felt as you do one day, walking in the old residence area. I went home and painted a picture of what I felt standing in the narrow street of that old neighborhood."

Nikolas was settled down simply by listening to Elena's voice.

Codros continued, "You are walking on ground and standing in water along a shore that people have occupied for thousands of years. You do not have this kind of history in California. For some people the history speaks to them. It's not unusual, enjoy it. Tell us about the ancient city's port."

Elena did just that as Nikolas paced back and forth in the water looking at his feet swirl and ripple the water of the Black Sea. When she had finished, Codros commented,

"I requested a table for us on the patio in the garden at noon. Do you think we will be back in time for lunch?"

Elena thought for a moment while Nikolas retrieved his shoes to continue their tour.

"We could visit St. Vladimir's Cathedral and then go back. The timing should be about right"

The three of them walked along the path leading up
the hill and crossed in front of the cathedral outside its
iron fence. They spent almost forty minutes in the
Cathedral. Codros purchased some candles and went off
on his own. Elena held on to Nikolas' arm to keep him
close, so her voice was not loud. He loved the frescoes
and the mosaics, and hearing the story of the structure.
Nikolas stood back by the entrance when Elena
purchased one candle for her father and lit it saying a
prayer and telling him how happy she was on this day.

Codros went outside and waited for Elena and her
attentive American tourist.

"Did you enjoy the Cathedral?"

Nikolas took a moment to allow his eyes to adjust to
the bright sunlight after being in the dimly lit Cathedral
before he answered Codros.

"Everything here has been touched by history."

They began their walk back to the hotel as Nikolas
continued,

"Somehow history reached out and touched me back
by the water. It's not just the ruins. You can process the
thought of people stacking stones to make a wall. But
when you touch a wall that has been touched for two
thousand three hundred and twenty years, it becomes an
emotional experience."

Elena was pleased to hear Nikolas express what she
had felt all her life. This man, this American man with a
Greek name, was very exhilarating.

Codros led the conversation during lunch allowing
Nikolas to drink in each and every comment or answer
Elena presented.

The smile never went away; it got larger sometimes but never left her face.

Her eyes were the most expressive. Nikolas watched them lead every change in her reactions to Codros.

Her laugh was warm and sincere, never forced. Elena's ease of conversation with Codros brought a great deal of joy to Nikolas.

The three continued to enjoy their lunch together until Codros apologized to both Elena and Nikolas, telling them he needed to spend a few hours on the phone with his family, or they may change the locks before he got home. Nikolas took the bill from the waiter when it came over Codros' strong objection. Nikolas reminded him who the customer was, and Codros thanked him for lunch and the refreshments before he said goodbye to Elena.

"He's a good man with an open heart. Treat him well and he will love you forever."

Codros was gone before Elena or Nikolas could recover from his comment. Elena turned back toward Nikolas with warmth in her expression that melted his heart.

"He is such a nice man. What do you think he sees that we don't?"

"Nothing, he's just honest enough to speak from his heart. What's next on my private tour of Chersonesus?"

As the two of them began their walk back through the hotel's gardens, Elena took Nikolas by the hand and redirected him toward what appeared to be a long white tent along the bluff. When they came around the end of the pavilion, they were stopped by an armed guard.

Elena spoke to the guard in Russian, and the young man let them pass.

It was like stepping into the world of National Geographic. For more than one hundred meters they were peeling back the surface of the land. Some of the areas had been sectioned off like a giant grid, and more digging was taking place.

"They found artifacts when they began to dig the footings for the cabana rooms along the bluff. All construction was stopped, and the search for artifacts and any signs of structures has begun," Elena explained.

"Incredible! How far back do they think the site will go?"

"No one is sure yet. It seems to be outside the protection of Chersonesus. Some of the artifacts found already predate the Greek city."

"That's more than two thousand five hundred years ago."

"Possibly. I wanted you to see this before we returned to our tour. We'll start in the two museums that display the artifacts found all through Chersonesus. Then we will walk the streets together, and I can describe the different areas of the ancient city. We should end up back at the hotel about five PM."

"Lead the way."

Elena thanked the guard and took Nikolas by the hand and led him through every room of the two museum buildings, the mint, the winery, all the outside structures and neighborhoods, exploring every detail and facet of life in the ancient city.

They ended the day at the site of the Roman Basilica. As they stood next to one of the columns looking back at the site, Elena asked, "What do you think of our city?"

"I've had an experience today that shall remain with me for the rest of my life. I've felt more alive walking through this city's ruins with you than at any other moment I can remember."

Nikolas saw the acknowledgment he was looking for in Elena's face.

"Can you join me to watch the sunset?"

"I would love to share a sunset with a man from the west with a Greek name."

Elena walked Nikolas back to the gardens and noticed the hotel had set up the bar and a few tables for the guests that enjoyed being outside.

"Would you like to enjoy your first sunset from the garden?"

They picked the table farthest away from the others, and Elena ordered for them. When she had finished she asked, "You must be tired?"

"I'm quite relaxed but at the same time too excited to be sleepy. What about you?"

"I've been talking all day, and I want to hear your voice. I'm tired of mine." Elena smiled and the conversation paused as the waitress served them.

"Start at the beginning: I, Nikolas Sebastian, was born... You know what I want to hear."

"I, Nikolas Sebastian, was born in a small town in Southern California.

"I...", and Nikolas told her his story with the ease of bringing an old friend up to date after not seeing one another for many years.

The two of them could not take their eyes off each other even for the sunset. Somehow it slipped past their view. They were the only two left, and Elena was actually a little cool. Nikolas noticed the shiver.

"I'm so sorry, you're cold."

"A little, perhaps it's time to go."

"Dinner? Have dinner with me. I'm not ready for you to go. I just found you a few hours ago."

"You are very sweet, and I must say, I have been hoping you would ask me to dinner. I feel as you do. This whole day has been such a joy for me. I do not want it to end. Why don't we take some time to get ready for dinner? I'll think about a restaurant you might like and meet you in the lobby one hour from now.

"Do I need to dress up"?

"No, I am a denim person most of the time."

Nikolas signed the check, and they walked quietly to the entrance of the hotel. They didn't know how to say goodbye and both laughed.

Elena found her words first, "We'll be together again in less than an hour. See you in the lobby, and you can tell me about your work at dinner."

"See you soon." He watched her until she disappeared into the darkness of the gardens.

Nikolas was walking toward the elevator lobby when he noticed Codros sitting alone in the small lobby bar. He decided to join him for a moment. As he approached, he realized he was on his cell phone. The stately Greek man noticed his approach and motioned him over to his table. Once Nikolas was seated, Codros must have said goodbye as he closed and set down his cell phone.

WISDOM

"If facts are the seeds that later produce knowledge and wisdom, then the emotions and the impressions of the senses are the fertile soil in which the seeds must grow."

~ Rachel Carson ~

"How was your day?"

"She's amazing."

"Did you enjoy Chersonesus?"

"The history's so rich, and somehow I feel connected to the city and most especially the harbor."

"Do you feel connected to your guide?"

"I've never met anyone quite like her. She seems as comfortable with me as I do with her. It's like we've known each other for a long time. She is an incredibly beautiful person inside and out."

"Where is she taking you for dinner?"

"I'm not sure, but I know we'll enjoy the dinner as much as our day. Join us, please. I hate thinking of you here alone."

"That was my wife I hung up on. And she expects a call back. Thank you for the invitation, but I must prepare for tomorrow. I'll see you Tuesday. Go, get ready for dinner, the rest of your life will be standing before you soon. Just remember, part of who she is has come from this place; she will not leave it for any long period of time. Respect her love for you as much as you respect your work. I'm very happy for you, Nikolas."

Codros had caught Nikolas off guard again with his insight and directness.

"I hope with all my heart your insights are correct. This young woman means more to me after a few hours than any other woman in my life. If I have any fear, it's the fear that I may be consumed by my feelings for her."

"You just need to let her in."

Nikolas thanked him again for the opportunity and the next few days. Codros' only response was, "Go, go enjoy every moment you share with Elena. I'll see you Tuesday morning and expect to see you both at breakfast."

Codros waited until Nikolas disappeared into the elevator lobby before he called his wife back.

"Mama, another American's heart has been stolen by a Ukraine woman."

IMPRESSIONS

*"Anyone can catch your eye, but it takes
someone special to catch your heart."*

~Author Unknown ~

Elena was standing near a taxi when Nikolas walked out of the lobby.

"Did I keep you waiting?"

"Not at all. I thought men were faster than women getting ready for dinner?"

"I ran into Codros in the lobby, and we talked for a few moments. You look stunning, by the way."

"Thank you."

Her denims were very faded and warn.

Her blouse was a darker blue and fit snugly, with small snaps from top to bottom, she had combed the bangs of her light blond hair straight down making her eyes greener and her lips redder.

Nikolas opened the door to the taxi and climbed in behind her. She had picked a restaurant that sat on the point inside Sevastopol's main harbor close to the ferry landing. She had reserved an outside table with a view across the small ferry inlet as well as a view across the bay toward the old cannon fortifications from the Crimean War. Elena ordered dinner for them and directed her attention back to Nikolas.

"I want to know about your work. I'm fascinated by sailing vessels."

Nikolas spent the next couple of hours talking about his education, his first job and his current work as an independent designer. Elena kept eye contact through their dinner and his discussion of work. When Nikolas took a break to eat a little, Elena and he would smile each time they looked up from their food. Nikolas was feeling so comfortable with Elena. He didn't want the evening to end.

After his explanation of what brought him to Sevastopol, he finished the last few bites of dinner as Elena had finished quite some time before him. When he looked up, Nikolas found Elena's sweet face looking back at him.

"What did Codros say to you in the lobby?"

Once again Nikolas was caught unprepared for the question. He looked down at his empty plate searching for the words to answer.

She continued, "Do you believe in fate? Do you understand how important you have become in my life in less than a day? Nikolas, look at me."

Nikolas raised his head.

His eyes were once again met by her smile and her eyes, so large and full of life. Nikolas was having a hard time controlling his emotions.

"I have my answer in your face, Nikolas. I can see your heart through your eyes, and you need to know I feel the same way. Let's go. I need to refresh my lipstick while you pay our bill. We can walk for a little bit and see what we decide to do later."

They left the patio and walked around the ferry landing and up the hill to the main street in Sevastopol city center. She turned right to show him the one American influence in town other than the hotel.

It was a McDonalds. On the wide sidewalk in front was a statue of Ronald himself.

They laughed and told each other silly youth stories about girls and boys as they walked not caring where they were going.

Nikolas and Elena were in constant contact with one another through holding hands or Elena holding Nikolas' arm.

The two had walked a considerable distance before they realized it was quite late.

Elena spotted a cab and negotiated a price in Russian before they got in. Nikolas was transitioning from joy to sorrow. He knew their day was over.

She recognized the change, as she was feeling the same way.

"It's my turn to extend an invitation. Would you like to come to my flat and see how the local people live in Sevastopol?"

Nikolas was elated by the invitation.

"Thank you, I would love to!"

When they reached her building, Nikolas paid the driver in dollars and they walked in silence to the building entrance. Elena opened the door and told Nikolas her flat was on the third floor. Once inside, she locked the door behind them.

"Please sit." Elena was gesturing toward the sofa in the small living room.

"Would you like some tea?"

Nikolas answered as he sat on the sofa,

"Yes please. Are the watercolors yours?"

Elena placed the teapot on the stove before she answered,

"Yes, the ones I want to keep are hung on my walls; the others, stacked in the corner, will be delivered to a gallery in the city center and sold."

"I love your work. This one with the open window and the Greek ship. Was it painted around here?" Nikolas heard the whistle of the teapot and turned his attention to Elena in the kitchen area. The flat was tastefully decorated but quite small.

"No, the image has always been in my imagination. As long ago as I can remember; it is my favorite picture."

"I can understand why. It's simply beautiful and so peaceful."

"Here's your tea. Careful, it's hot." Elena sat close to Nikolas.

"Your flat is beautiful and cozy."

"I've heard how big your houses are. I know my home is small, but I like it."

"I feel very comfortable here."

"Then you should stay."

Elena leaned over and kissed his cheek, "By the time we finish our tea and talk a little longer, it will be 4:00 AM. I do not want you to go, how do you feel?"

"I feel like my life has changed dramatically and for the better in less than a day. I can only credit you for the change, and I don't want to leave you and wake in my bed in California, with all of this nothing more than a dream."

Elena smiled and pinched him on his thigh, "You're not dreaming, and I could not stand to watch you walk out the door. I owe you a childhood description, and then we go to sleep."

"Please."

They sat for about an hour talking about her childhood up to the point both of them were almost asleep sitting on the sofa holding hands. Elena shook his hand to get his attention.

"I'll find you a toothbrush, and I'll clean up a little, OK?"

Nikolas shook his head in acknowledgment and followed Elena into the small bedroom.

She leaned him against the doorway of the tiny bathroom while she looked for a toothbrush.

Nikolas took the brush and replaced Elena in the bathroom. He finished and turned to see the covers on the left side of the bed had been laid back. Elena came in from the living room and retrieved what looked like pajamas from the armoire and went into the bathroom, closing the door. Nikolas stripped down to his boxers, folded his clothes, set them on the floor next to the bed and got under the sheet and the single cover. Elena reentered the bedroom and put her clothes away before she got into bed dressed in her flannel pajamas. She switched the light off and turned toward Nikolas.

"Can you sleep with the window open?"

"I love a soft breeze and a kiss goodnight."

"Then come here and I'll give you just one kiss to go to sleep with."

Nikolas did what he was told, except the one kiss lasted a very long time. When they stopped, their hearts were racing. Nikolas took her hand and placed it on his heart. Elena responded by placing his hand on her heart.

"Sleep, Nikolas, tomorrow is our second day, and I want both of us to dream about what will happen."

JOURNEY

"I love you, not only for what you are,
but for what I am when I am with you."

~ Roy Croft ~

It wasn't quite daylight when Nikolas woke.

He couldn't help think about Codros' words.

Nikolas was up on his left side just looking at Elena as she slumbered.

What would he say to her subconscious mind if he could?

Nikolas took a few more moments to drink in the sight in front of his eyes and lying next to him.

He began to form the words he would pass on if he could.

"As I lie in bed with you, so much runs through my mind. I ask myself, how did I come to this moment in time? I lie here on one side, gazing at you while you sleep so contently on your back. You are motionless except for your rhythmic breathing. Only your face and

neck are exposed to the early morning air. The rising sun is removing the shadows that cover you ever so slowly bringing a final clarity to my view.

How lucky I am to see you undisturbed by any outside influence including myself. The marvel is the smile I see on your face. Your full lips are not parted, and the smile is not nearly as broad as it is when you're at your happiest during the day. But something so wonderfully captivating surrounds you in your sleep. Your beautiful green eyes may be closed, but they seem just as large and only resting before they take in another wonderful day.

My first instinct is to kiss your lips and try to feel the peace you must be experiencing. I can't bring myself to do that because I know you will wake and lose the beauty and the innocence that surrounds you sleep. I love you, Elena. Somehow, in this early morning light, words simply are not enough."

Once all the shadows had been removed from the room, and the all the birds were singing their songs, Nikolas saw Elena's eyes slowly open to the new day.

She was pleased to see Nikolas smiling back at her.

Elena reached out with both arms and gently pulled Nikolas to her for a good morning kiss.

"Good morning, have you been awake for long?"

"Just long enough to watch you sleeping. You look quite happy and peaceful when you sleep."

"I should be happy and peaceful; I've found the man I've been looking for all my life."

Elena's arms were still around Nikolas' neck and she gently pulled him closer again kissing him until her heart started racing once more.

Nikolas realized her arms were bare. It must have been too hot for flannel during the night.

Elena stretched and pulled the sheet back up to her neck, and rolled over on her right side to face Nikolas.

"We should plan our day."

"We could stay in bed all day."

"We could, but you are not here long, and I want you to see more of Sevastopol. I also need to deliver my paintings to the gallery."

"Can I help?"

"I was counting on your help."

Elena smiled thinking how comfortable she was with this man from eleven thousand kilometers away. She hoped her second day would be as fulfilling as her first.

"You go back to California on Wednesday?"

"Yes."

"When do you meet Codros again?"

"We meet the metal treatment people Tuesday morning."

"Then we have all of today and tomorrow if I take the day off."

"Could you?"

"I believe I can. Would you like to stay with me rather than in the hotel?"

"I would love to. I was hoping you would ask."

"I think it would be best if you checked out. Sevastopol is a small town in some ways."

"I understand. I should go back, clean up, pack and check out. I could be back in an hour or so and help with your paintings. What do you think?"

"We may do a little sight-seeing before we go to the gallery, and I'll think about that before you return."

"Sounds great."

Elena leaned forward and kissed him before she turned on her other side to get out of bed.

"The keys are on the kitchen counter. You will need them to lock the door to the flat when you leave and to get back in. Don't look. It was too hot for flannel last night. See you soon. Don't look, I'm a little shy."

Nikolas watched as she slid out of bed with her arms held close to her gorgeous body, and her hands must have been covering her breasts. She was beautiful in her lace panties. Once behind the protection of the bathroom door she looked around with a childish expression,

"You looked!"

"You're as beautiful outside as you are inside."

Elena's expression changed to gratitude.

"Thank you, your turn."

Nikolas didn't need to be so shy. He tossed the covers back to reveal his boxers and stood up posing like a muscleman first on his right side and then on his left. Elena laughed.

"You're beautiful and so fit." She laughed again, "Come here and kiss me good bye."

Nikolas happily responded, and gave Elena another long kiss, exciting both of them.

After he packed, he wrote a note to leave for Codros, advising him that he had checked out and would call later with a local number when he picked up a chip for his cell phone.

Nikolas sat at the desk for a few moments thinking about all the emotion he had felt since he met Elena.

It was like all his life was suddenly restarted.

He had a reason to wake up each day and share his day with someone who was truly interested in his feelings, not just theirs.

He decided he should send an e-mail to his mom and dad about meeting Elena and his almost spiritual experiences at Chersonesus.

Elena was standing in front of her small bathroom mirror looking at her own expression. She was realizing everything she had wanted, but the image in the mirror told her she was worried.

Her dream last night had been very short, but the images were the most vivid she had ever seen. She was just a witness to her dream, not a participant. A small ancient Greek ship, like the one in her painting in the living room, was leaving Chersonesus harbor. The boat was being rowed rather than sailed quite a distance off shore, and then it turned east. Nightfall turned to daybreak, and the small trading vessel was under sail. What seemed like moments later, a larger ship appeared and overtook the much smaller craft from Chersonesus.

The crew on the small ship seemed frightened, and Elena saw a shower of arrows coming toward the little ship. Her next image was of a man collapsing in front of her. As he did, she saw the face of Nikolas on the dying man who had been struck by several arrows.

She had no idea what the dream could mean and had no idea how all this could happen in one day?

The joy of meeting the man she had been waiting for all her life and the unanswered question about the meaning of the small trading ship and Nikolas dying in her dream... This was the confusion she saw in the mirror.

But what did her mom say? "Sometimes you can't find an explanation for a feeling or a purpose…" Elena looked in the mirror again and said to herself, *"Finish your makeup and simply enjoy the day with a man that seems to have the same feelings for you."*

Nikolas checked out and left the note for Codros. When he reached her apartment, the door was ajar and he went in. Elena had prepared breakfast for them and was finishing with the tea when Nikolas came into her flat.

"Put your suitcase in the bedroom and come to breakfast. You did not eat, did you?"

"I didn't. I'm hungry."

"Come sit, I'll tell you what we will do today."

Nikolas deposited his suitcase in the bedroom and returned to the small kitchen, dining room table.

"Thank you for asking me to stay."

"You're very welcome. I've never played house before. You're my first male roommate."

"I'm flattered." Nikolas was admiring his new roommate. She had the denims from last night on with a new blouse that was just as fitted as the one she had worn. Elena had changed to sport shoes from boots. She just looked amazing in anything she put on. Nikolas' admiration did not go unnoticed and was met with her wonderful warm smile.

They finished breakfast, talking about how they could bundle up her paintings without harming them, and where he could get a chip for his phone.

They were planning their day as if they'd lived with each other for years, at the same time the excitement about this new relationship was causing shy smiles and constant touching.

Nikolas placed the bundled paintings very carefully into the taxi when it came to pick them up. The unloading went quickly with help from the owner of the gallery. She was quite nice and seemed rather happy to receive Elena's latest works. Elena took Nikolas' arm, guided him across the street and headed them toward the avenue they'd walked up the night before from the ferry landing.

Elena stopped them in front of a store that sold cell phones and accessories. With her help, Nikolas purchased a chip and a card with a code for time. Their next stop was a hotel just a block away. Elena spoke with the driver of the next taxi that pulled in to drop a passenger.

Nikolas was about to get in when Elena said,

"No, Nikolas. He's too expensive. We need to wait a moment."

Nikolas stepped back on the curb and decided to call Codros and give him his cell number while Elena selected a cab.

The taxi ride to the park where the Museum of Panorama was located didn't take long. They walked up the broad pathway and started the climb of a series of steps when Elena began her description of the Crimean War and the significance of the position they were walking on. When she paused, Nikolas commented,

"We need a camera."

"They have wonderful photo sets for sale in the Museum."

"I want some photos of us today."

"Look at the small vendor stands as we pass. One will certainly have disposable cameras."

Nikolas found a vendor and purchased two cameras. The merchant was pleased enough to photograph the couple in front of her stand. Elena held onto Nikolas' arm and leaned her head on his shoulder. Nikolas smiled and waved at the camera.

As expected, the Panorama building was large and round. They paid for the entrance and climbed the stairs that took them up to the viewing area.

Elena held Nikolas close to her, like she had in the museum buildings the day before, and quietly explained the different scenes as they slowly worked their way around the gallery.

It was a reproduction of the Crimean War and the defense of Sevastopol that took place between 1854 and 1855; men dying for their country. Some of the stories Elena told of the bravery and the odd respect that came from one side of the battle to the other at times which made it a different kind of battle. Respect and war was an odd concept for Nikolas. Perhaps Elena was right. It was the last war fought with honor. This Panorama drove home the point of how little he actually knew of the rest of the world.

"I want to show you some of the actual gun emplacements that protected Sevastopol from invasion."

They walked toward the hillside behind the Panorama and toured the emplacements that still existed. The view was commanding, and it was easy to understand why it had been difficult to assault. Elena continued her discussion of the site's history as they walked. She had a far better understand of her city's two thousand five hundred year history than he had of LA's two hundred and fifty year history. Nikolas had asked another tourist to take their photo standing next to one of the large field mortars and offered to take theirs in exchange. Elena admired how outgoing he was and also innocent. The sky had a few clouds beginning to form, and Elena wanted to take Nikolas to Balaklava before the rain began; she needed a taxi.

Guiding Nikolas away from the hillside, she directed them toward a narrow street. It would take them to the amusement park below the hillside they had just been standing on. When they passed the ball toss with the big stuffed bears as a prize, Nikolas tried to get her to stop.

"We can come back another day. I think you will love Balaklava. It is an ancient harbor that has developed quite nicely, and the food and views are wonderful."

"You're the guide, but I love teddy bears."

Nikolas was looking over his shoulder like a little boy being led away from the arcade. Elena had the warmest feeling for this man that walked into her life just one day before.

FRIENDSHIP

*"A friend is someone with whom you
dare to be yourself."*

~ Frank Crane ~

The taxi dropped them in the turnaround right by one of the restaurants with patio seating. Once inside, Elena spoke to the hostess for a moment before they were seated outside. Nikolas was admiring Elena more than the collection of yachts, commercial and military vessels just behind her in the harbor.

Elena began to tell Nikolas about the British occupation of the harbor during the Crimean War. Nikolas, interrupting her, leaned across the table and kissed her on the lips.

Sitting back down he said, "You are such a beautiful woman on such a beautiful day. I just want to look at you and talk to you. I love your city, but I love you more."

Nikolas felt Elena's leg rub against his and a smile cover her face.

"I'll stop being a guide through lunch if you tell me about your mother and father."

"You promise not to be bored?"

"If I know them, I will know you better."

The waitress came and took their order from Elena. Nikolas talked about his Mom and Dad for some time before Elena asked a question.

"Did you miss your father in between trips sailing?"

"Yes, I did. He wasn't around much for t-ball, little league and soccer. He wasn't around for graduation from middle school or high school. I always got a call or two each week, but mom filled the gap most of the time. I don't resent it. I just don't know what it would have been like to have him around. What about your father?"

"He died when I was nine, almost ten years old. I still remember him, and you helped me carry the result of his impact on me into the gallery today. My mother had to be both parents, but I missed my father, growing up. Tell me more about your mother."

Nikolas had finished his late lunch and ordered an espresso before he told her about his mother's strength. As he finished, Elena checked the time and thought it was quite late for them to make the fortress before the sky was clouded over. She knew it would be raining soon.

"We need to restart our tour if we expect to make it up to the fortress before it gets too cold for us."

"Can we just walk a little? I'd like to see the boats, and perhaps you can show me the fortress from a distance if it's too late. We may get wet if we go too far."

"I forget, you're a sailor and know the weather. Let's take a leisurely stroll to the end of the walkway."

Elena went to the restroom while Nikolas paid the bill. He wanted to see the small marina next to the restaurant before they started their walk.

"There are some nice power yachts here. Does Balaklava have a shipyard?"

"I believe it does on the other side of the marina. You see the military vessels?"

"Yes."

"What you can't see from here is the small shipyard behind the military ships. We might be able to look back and see it from the other end of the walkway."

Nikolas took Elena's hand and they began their walk past the freshly restored buildings with shops, bars and restaurants on the first floor and small hotels or flats on the second and third floors.

On the other side of the broad grey and red brick walkway was Balaklava's protected harbor.

It was a beautiful sight.

"Nikolas, look up on the hill."

He looked in the direction of Elena's outstretched arm.

"It's the Genoese fortress. It's amazing!"

Nikolas looked for someone to take their photo and showed an older man out for his afternoon stroll how to use the camera.

He posed himself and Elena just as it started to rain.

The gentleman took the photo Nikolas had wanted and another photo of them with their arms raised and smiling at each other as it began to rain harder.

Nikolas thanked the man as Elena tugged on his hand to head for shelter.

They ran back to the restaurant and went inside.

Elena used Nikolas' cell to call a taxi.

"We will have some time to wait. It has been raining in Sevastopol for a little longer, and the taxis are busy."

"We have time for a glass of wine?"

"We should. I love to watch the rain on the water." They stood at the small bar until the glasses were poured and moved to a table next to the window. Sitting at the table, Nikolas remembered he had put his hat in one of the cargo pockets of his shorts. Elena was peacefully looking out the window, watching the raindrops splash into the harbor, thinking how easy it was spending time with Nikolas.

"Are you here or someplace else?"

"I am with you and thinking how comfortable I feel and how... I do not know, at peace I feel. I haven't thought of any of the issues that bother me sometimes. I haven't had a thought other than how comfortable..."

"Excuse me, sir. Your hat. Is that "Breeze", the Maxi Boat?"

Elena and Nikolas were a little startled by the clarity of English coming from the bartender.

"Yes, it is."

"Do you crew on her?"

Elena, with a great deal of pride, answered,

"No, he is the marine architect that designed the boat."

The bartender came around the small bar to the side of their table.

"You're Nikolas Sebastian?"

"Yes, I am."

The bartender extended his hand and introduced himself.

"I'm Aleksi Nikitin, and I'm a great admirer of your work. I heard Codros Theophilus was in town with his designer."

"You're well informed."

"No need to worry. We aren't spying. I may own the restaurant but don't make the money to race a maxi." Mr. Nikitin's smile was very broad and Nikolas laughed at the comment before he responded.

"I'm not recognized in Southern California often, and I am most flattered to be recognized here, in Balaklava. This is a friend of mine, Elena Andreev." Aleksi shook her hand.

"You are a lucky person to know this man. He is an artist."

"I know how lucky I am and thank you. You have a wonderful restaurant."

Aleksi thanked Elena in Russian and told her their money was no good in his restaurant as they were now his guests. Elena thanked him in Russian and asked him in English to join them while they waited for a taxi. Aleksi accepted the invitation and sat down with them before he addressed Nikolas.

Elena watched the two men, divided by half the world, enjoy a discussion of a sport both were passionate about. Nikolas was the first to laugh and tease Aleksi who was quite willing to return the teasing at the right moment. Elena had forgotten about the taxi and didn't hear the horn honk for them. When the driver entered the restaurant, he was upset as it was now raining quite hard. Aleksi excused himself and talked with the driver until he was settled down. Returning, he shook Nikolas' hand.

"Please come any time. I enjoyed our conversation, and I'm sure we can find a boat for you to sail on for one of our race weekends." He turned to Elena, "I'm so sorry I ignored you. It was quite rude. We don't get too many people like Nikolas in Balaklava. Again, I'm sorry."

"It was my pleasure watching two grown boys talk of a sport they are so fervent about. I am sure we will see you again."

Aleksi gave Elena a card for the restaurant and walked them to the door.

The ride back to Elena's flat was slow and quite. It was almost dark out at 4:00 PM, and they could see lightning and hear the thunder. The two of them got soaked running from the front of Elena's building to the backside where her entrance was.

Once in her apartment, Elena directed Nikolas, "Please take your clothes off here, in the entry and take a warm shower."

"You go first."

"I'll get a beach towel and be dry before you're in the shower, please."

Nikolas complied with her request. Once he was warm, he got out and dried off.

"Elena! I'm out, your turn."

When he came out, Elena was standing by the door, wrapped in a beach towel, looking a little cold. She went in, and the shower was running again warming her from head to toe. Nikolas finished drying in the bedroom, noticing the windows had been closed, and a towel was on the hardwood floor, soaking up water. The bed was turned down on his side, inviting him to get under the covers. Nikolas finished drying off the floor after he had put clean boxers on. He took the wet towel to the kitchen and placed it in the sink along with their soaked clothing. Nikolas returned to the bedroom just before he heard the water turned off and got under the covers. He heard Elena.

"Are you warmer?"

"I'm under the covers and waiting for you to warm me."

"I'll be right there." Elena came out of the bathroom with her hair wrapped in a towel, with a gorgeous lace bra and panty set on. His eyes told Elena she had picked the right set. In a flash she was under the covers on her side with her back to Nikolas.

"What is the English word when two people are close in bed?"

"Snuggle."

"Snuggle me"

"Snuggle with me."

Elena smiled and felt Nikolas' body conform to hers like spoons in a drawer. Her heart was racing in a matter of seconds. Her whole body was excited about his closeness, his touch. Elena took his hand and placed it on her heart.

"Elena."

"You do excite me so quickly. It is almost as if my body knew what to expect. Hold me closer."

Nikolas pulled her closer and kissed the back of her neck and felt a little involuntary reaction in her right leg.

"Tell me about your first girlfriend."

Nikolas and Elena talked about childhood girlfriends and boyfriends as the lightning lit up the room, and the thunder rattled the windows. Nikolas was the first to fall asleep. Elena was not asleep long before she began dreaming of a young woman sitting in front of an easel in ancient times. She had recognized the painting she was working on. It was just like the one on the wall of her own living room: a small trading ship coming into Chersonesus.

The woman in her dream was dressed in warm clothing, looked very much like her, and the room appeared to be small, like her bedroom. She seemed to be very upset, crying as she painted.

KISS ME A THOUSAND TIMES

"A kiss is a lovely trick designed by nature to stop speech when words become superfluous."

~ Ingrid Bergman ~

Elena was up early and on the phone with Yasha, her manager at the hotel.

She had told him she needed to take the day off, and Yasha had understood. Elena had also called Dimitre and thankfully went to voice mail at his office. She asked him to call her Tuesday morning at her office. Her third call was to a driver she wanted to hire for the day and a surprise for her new roommate. Finished with her calls, Elena had time to think before she returned to bed and Nikolas.

Many of her previous dreams of ancient times had repeated time and time again.

Her last two had never appeared in the past.

She could not dismiss that they were telling her something about Nikolas and herself.

143

The problem was what they were trying to tell her.

She was cold when she finally snuggled up to Nikolas, and he woke turning toward her.

He placed his arm over her shoulder and pulled her close to him.

Elena could feel him the entire length of her body.

He had excited her simply by touching her.

His eyes were not open all the way; he was still half asleep when he spoke, "Good morning, roommate."

Nikolas kissed her neck below her chin, once, twice and a third time.

Elena's body responded positively after the second caress.

She wanted to continue, but Elena also wanted a day or two more, just to make sure.

"I have a surprise for you." Elena's voice was a little breathy. Nikolas was fully awake when he answered, "I love surprises."

He slowly ran his hand down her side and ending at the center of her lower back, holding her very close to him.

"The first surprise is breakfast because I am very hungry. The second surprise is I have the day off, and the third surprise is we are going to have a picnic lunch together at a place, I know, you will love."

"Do we need to get up now?"

"I do, you don't."

"I need to get up, too. I want to see you and talk to you. I love your thong. Is it OK to be attracted to you physically?"

"I would hope you are. I'm attracted to you physically."

Elena ran her hand down his side and then under his boxers squeezing his bottom. They both laughed, and she got out of bed again. Elena took her sheer robe from the armoire and he found a t-shirt in his suitcase. She went to the kitchen and Nikolas to the bathroom. After he had brushed his teeth, he heard Elena.

"Breakfast is ready."

Nikolas sat at the small table already set with fresh fruit and yogurt and waited for Elena to finish pouring juice. She set a glass next to his fruit bowl and sat down.

"Do you like long walks?"

Nikolas was admiring Elena again. Actually he could not take his eyes off of her sitting across from him. Her robe was open, and he could see how beautiful her unblemished skin was.

"Nikolas?"

"I'm sorry."

"What were you thinking about?"

"You."

"You're sweet, thank you. Do you like long walks?"

"I love to walk. Where are we going?

"It's a surprise. One, I know, you will like, and we will have lunch on top of the world."

145

They finished breakfast, and Nikolas volunteered to do dishes while Elena got ready. When it was Nikolas' turn, Elena retrieved her old backpack and loaded it with bottled water, salami, cheese, half of a baguette and some condiments. Their walk would be quite long and strenuous the last half kilometer. Elena told Nikolas to wear his shorts, a t-shirt and a sweater or sweatshirt. Nikolas emerged from the bedroom, and Elena handed him the backpack.

"Our driver is here. Are you ready?"

"I need a camera."

"In the outside pocket of the backpack."

"I'm excited about the surprise and our third day together."

Elena took his hand and opened the door with the same warm feelings in her heart as well.

The drive wasn't too long. The driver spoke English and was happy to point out unique land features and historic monuments along the way, relieving Elena of her Crimean guide responsibilities. When they pulled into a small community and came to the end of the street, Elena told the driver they would be back in three or four hours and gave him Nikolas' cell number.

Their walk started on a path that would lead them through a narrowing canyon before it opened out to a rising meadow and revealed the ancient fortress. Elena began to tell him about the Uspensky Cave Monastery they would pass on the way to their lunch site.

Elena watched Nikolas look at everything she talked about along the way. He was so fascinated, like a child.

It helped her to deliver the stories with great enthusiasm and detail.

Nikolas was in awe of the Cave Monastery. He was literally drinking in all the history around him, and at the center was this beautiful spirit holding his arm and guiding him through a wonderland.

Elena knew the Monastery and the topography would move him, she had no idea he would become this involved until she saw the tears fall from her roommate's eyes.

"Would you like to sit for a few minutes?"

"I'm sorry, it's just overpowering to think of the people, the civilizations, and the time that has passed here. And you... I'm just overwhelmed. How many people have walked on this path? How many people have been born here, died here? It's all too overpowering. Can we keep moving?"

Elena and Nikolas continued up the path past local vendors, and wooded areas with people offering horseback rides before Nikolas spoke.

"What was it like for you to grow up here?"

Elena thought for a moment.

"We had to learn more history than you did."

Nikolas smiled at Elena.

"I'm sorry, I was so emotional by the Monastery."

"Many years and many people have past that spot, and it has a very strong impact on some people. I'm glad you could feel the energy and the emotion. You have a good heart."

The trail was getting a little steeper and filled with a few more obstacles. Elena and Nikolas walked single file for some time. When they emerged from the woods, Nikolas could see several structures on top of a high plateau.

"Where are we?"

"We're almost to Chufut-Kale which means Jewish Fortress. Are you hungry yet?"

"I'm OK, it's amazing from here."

"If you can wait, we will eat on top. It is not as close as you think, and the trail is quite steep."

Looking up once more, the only clouds he could see were the contrails left by a passing airliner. They made their way up the balance of the trail to what Elena told Nikolas was the back entrance to the fortified settlement. It was originally occupied in the eighth and ninth century. She led him to a spot on the far side of the site that had a commanding view across a wide valley to another high plateau. It was quite a spectacular site. Nikolas took off the backpack and found the camera. With no one around to take pictures of the two of them together, he took several photos of Elena with the fortress and the expanse between the two plateaus as her background. The lunch topic continued to be the site, they were sitting on, and the Monastery.

Rested and ready to continue, Nikolas stood and offered his hand to Elena.

Her smile was inviting as she stood, and Nikolas stepped closer and kissed her.

When she didn't break off the kiss, he pulled her close and continued the caress until his heart was once again racing, and his desires were building within him.

Elena was swept away by his embrace and became quite weak in his arms.

She was now positive: this was the man she had been dreaming of since she was a child. She only needed to know for sure he was feeling the same way.

When they finished, they were both a little embarrassed to see a few people with gentle smiles, watching them.

Nikolas took a bow as if he were an actor on stage. Holding Elena's hand up, he gestured toward her with his free hand and then bowed again bringing on applause from the audience. That caused Elena to join in and bow, and the applause become even louder. Nikolas was laughing when he wrapped his arms around Elena once again and gave her a brief kiss. The audience moved on, as did Elena and Nikolas. The walk around the plateau didn't take them as long as Elena had expected, and the trip back to the Monastery was a quiet handholding walk.

While Elena was filling their empty water bottle at the Monastery's legendary spring, Nikolas finished the roll of film in one of the cameras.

Elena used the cell phone to tell the driver they would meet him in just a few minutes. The ride back was very quiet until Elena asked, "Would you like to eat in or go out to dinner?"

"I'm not terribly hungry. Could we eat in?"

"A light dinner?"

"Yes, please, at your place."

The focus of Nikolas' eyes drifted out of the car as his mind once again reviewed the last few days. It was the first time he began to feel the reality of work beginning in the morning and the trip back home. He couldn't think of going home. When he turned toward Elena, she was smiling back at him.

She kissed his cheek and said, "Don't think about tomorrow or the next day. We have each other and we have tonight."

Nikolas' expression changed in an instant, and the kiss on the cheek brought back a smile.

Elena instructed the driver to take them to a specific grocery store and wait for them. They went into the store hand in hand, and Elena asked, "Can you pick out some fruit, and I will pick up salad ingredients?"

Nikolas acknowledged and went to the other end of the produce section of the small store. Everything looked fresh, and he picked out some berries and rejoined Elena. She was looking over the various heads of lettuce and picked out one that looked like romaine.

"I'm glad you like fresh berries."

"I'm glad you like romaine."

They laughed and looked over the tomatoes together.

Elena wished they could shop every night for their dinner, and it was her turn to look a little sad.

"Remember what you said in the car?"

"Yes, I do. Are we ready?"

"I am, I want to be alone with you."

"Let's go then."

When they opened the door to Elena's flat, Nikolas' phone rang.

"Nikolas, it's Codros."

"Hello, sorry I haven't called."

"We've missed you here at the hotel. Have you enjoyed the sightseeing?"

"We just returned from the Cave Monastery and Chufut-Kale."

"You have been busy."

As the two men discussed what they would accomplish the next day, Elena took the groceries to her small kitchen and washed the fruit and vegetables, setting them out to dry. She kissed Nikolas on the cheek as she passed on her way to the bathroom. She hurried because she knew he would not be on the phone call much longer.

Nikolas heard the water turn off, and he told Codros they could continue the conversation over coffee at 8:30 as their appointment was at 10:00.

When Elena reappeared, she only had a towel wrapped around her.

"You have time to freshen up while I make the salad"

Nikolas' kissed Elena's cheek and disappeared through the bedroom door. The early evening was warmer than the night before, and Elena had opened the bedroom windows and the doors to the small balcony off the living room. The breeze felt good to Nikolas, and he liked the gentle motion of the curtains. He had not been prepared to stay with anyone, so his only comfortable clothing option was a clean pair of boxers and a clean t-shirt. When he came back into the living room, the sun was beginning to set and two candles were glowing on the small dining table. Elena was at the kitchen counter in her sheer robe and matching bra and panties she had put on while he was in the shower. Nikolas came up behind her and put his arms around her waist, realizing that her robe was hanging open. Elena backed into him to be as close as she could to this wonderful man, saying, "Is my roommate all cleaned up?"

Nikolas kissed her neck and felt her reaction as she set her knife in the sink and turned toward Nikolas. Her bra and panties were as sheer as the robe, and Nikolas just looked at her before kissing her again. Elena put her arms around him under his t-shirt and pulled him closer. Elena could feel his excitement and slowed down the pace until they were both under control again.

"Dinner."

"Maybe a cold shower." They both laughed.

"Sit down please. It is just salad and a little sliced meat."

Nikolas sat facing the kitchen and watched Elena finished preparing their salad and placed it on the table along with some crackers, sliced prosciutto and the rest of the cheese left from lunch. Silence took over again and was not broken until Elena was seated and they began to eat. Nikolas raised a glass for a toast.

"To love at first sight, to family, however large or small, no matter where in the world they may be, and to you, Elena Andreev. Thank you for filling my life with more joy than I ever expected to find."

Elena lifted her glass.

"And to you, Nikolas Sebastian. I have been waiting for you all my life and cannot bear the thought of losing you the day after tomorrow."

Elena touched her glass to Nikolas' and tears began to fall from their eyes.

Elena got up from the table and went to the bedroom, embarrassed about her emotional outbreak.

Nikolas waited a moment to let her recover before he followed her in. She was sitting on the edge of the bed with her head down, but she had stopped crying.

Nikolas sat beside her and put one arm around her and reached over with the other and turned the light off before he spoke.

"I find it so much easier to talk with you when we're alone here, in your bedroom. I have no fear of loving you when we're in this room. I have no fear of expressing myself here. I have all the confidence I need to be honest and not hold back when I'm with you here. It's like we were standing before one another with nothing but our words to express our feelings. I know I must be more careful with my words. Because when I'm here with you, I know you hear each and every one of them, undisturbed by the world outside. I want you to understand how I feel about you, and how important you have become by asking one question. May I stay with you in your heart and in your home for one more week? Your roommate for another week."

Elena lifted her head, and Nikolas could see in the moonlight that her beautiful smile replaced the tears.

Elena reached around his neck with both arms and pulled him down on top of her as she fell back on the bed, whispering, "Kiss me a thousand times."

And he did.

PREMONITIONS

To love someone deeply gives you strength. Being loved by someone deeply gives you courage.

~ Lao Tzu ~

Nikolas said goodbye to Elena in the morning, took his computer and headed to the hotel and coffee with Codros. His head wasn't filled with sailboat specifications or next steps that needed to be taken; he could only think of the evening he and Elena had just spent together.

Their kissing had been passionate as was their touching, but again they both found their way back and needed to talk about life, family, children and the support, they felt, either one of them might need as the years together unfolded.

It was a discussion of the importance of a family rather than the individual.

The dedication to a family needed to survive in the world of broken marriages today. Nikolas had bared his feelings to the point of breaking down over the issue of his past failure. Elena had to remind him that two people made up a marriage.

He loved this woman with every fiber in his body in less than three days and felt as if he had known her for twenty years.

What would he do?

Codros watched Nikolas walk by as he took a sip of his coffee. He was seated near the coffee table the hotel put out early each morning. Almost laughing, Codros called out,

"Nikolas!"

The marine architect stopped and turned as his face flushed. Nikolas got a cup of coffee himself before sitting in a chair next to Codros.

"You may need to fire me and find someone new to finish the boat."

"You're kidding, my friend! I think I will have the first Sebastian designed boat that is not only engineered on the leading edge and a winner; this one will also have heart, lots of heart. How are you? You look a little lost but happy."

Nikolas took a moment and tried to find the right words for his client to hear. When he finely opened his mouth, his heart poured out instead.

"I can't find the words to thank you for bringing me here. Elena is the most wonderful, gentle, loving person I've ever met. I'll always be in your debt for the past three days, and I hope for her companionship for the rest of my life."

"I told my wife on Saturday the American women lost another fine man to a Ukrainian girl. The more I hear about Elena, the better I feel regarding what is happening between the two of you. She seems to be as creative as you are in addition to being as honest. I'm happy for you both."

"Elena couldn't join us for breakfast. She has a meeting with the developers here. Let's talk about this metal process."

Nikolas and Codros had two cups of coffee before the driver arrived in the lobby to take them to their meeting. On the way it was apparent that the weather was changing rather suddenly, as it had before.

They agreed that Codros would conduct the meeting to let Nikolas keep good notes and ask his questions toward the end of their time at the manufacturing facility. The test data, they made available, and the demonstrations of the end products flexibility and strength were impressive to Nikolas and Codros. Nikolas' questions were answered, and the Company's president asked if they would like to sail on their J 24 based demonstration boat.

Nikolas said, "I'm assuming you had a J 24 to collect all her measurements."

The Company's president answered,

"We still have the boat at our dock. J Boats actually sent an older boat to us, and we have used it as a trial horse. If the two of you sign a nondisclosure, we'll provide you with the results. It is quite interesting to see the performance difference, especially to weather."

They accepted the invitation for the sail and thanked the President for his time.

Elena went to work soon after Nikolas had left her flat. The hotel developer was anxious to receive her update on the archeologists' preliminary findings, regarding the area that was under excavation. She spent the morning reassuring the hotel developer that the site could be managed as an attraction for the hotel, to stimulate a higher level of occupancy in addition to its contribution to the understanding of local history.

Her meeting had ended after several hours and she needed to share the results of her discussions with the two senior archeologists at the site. Her afternoon would be full, and her day was progressing quickly, bringing her closer to spending time with Nikolas.

Nikolas had hoped to see Elena when they came back to the hotel. Codros needed to change his clothes and he took some time to call Elena's office. He was told she had been in a meeting all morning and it hadn't broken up yet. Nikolas left a message in her voice mail that he would be out sailing with his client all afternoon, and that they would like her to join them at the small lobby bar after work. Nikolas ended the message by saying he missed her already, and it was only lunchtime. Codros rejoined him, and they began their walk to the small marina on the bay behind Chersonesus.

Nikolas had noticed the worsening weather conditions from earlier in the day, and he was becoming concerned about it raining. As they walked, the two men talked of the advantages of this new material and also the problems they could face. They passed St. Vladimir Cathedral and were walking down the hill when Nikolas felt as if he had been here, sailed from here before.

They met the company's marketing director at the dock, and he showed them the boat. The hull, the spars and the rigging were an exact duplicate of a J 24. The small boat had been rigged and it was ready to sail including two sets of foul-weather gear in the cockpit.

Nikolas took note of the wind direction and told Codros they could sail directly from the dock. They were moving forward quite nicely as the main came into trim, and Codros began trimming the jib. Nikolas had Codros take the tiller once they were out of Chersonesus harbor, so he could inspect the construction. Nikolas wanted to sail into Sevastopol's main harbor, forcing them to do a fair amount of tacking. The worsening weather conditions would test the small boat's strength, as the wind had already risen above 15 knots.

After exercising the boat within Sevastopol's harbor Nikolas had Codros hold the boat into the wind as he reduced sail area in response to the increased wind velocity. They returned to the open sea for more testing before they headed back to Chersonesus.

Elena checked for messages following her morning meeting, and played the voice mail Nikolas had left for her several times, thinking at first how nice it was for him to care about her and her day. She needed to spend some time with the archeologists, explaining how important it was to their project to have the hotel benefit from their work. Her discussions were not going well until she reminded them they were digging on private property, and the city did not have the funds to purchase the site. They finally agreed to help the hotel owners create a site plan that would allow guests to view the active dig. With proper security, they also agreed that the cataloged pieces could be displayed in the hotel.

The afternoon was getting quite cold, and the wind was extremely strong by the time Elena finished her discussions.

She took a moment to look out to sea and saw how high the swells were. The wind seemed to be tearing the tops of the swells off and blowing them toward the beach. Elena remembered Nikolas and Codros had gone sailing on a small boat.

When one of the archeologists noticed her expression, he commented, "What's wrong?"

"Some friends went sailing."

"I hope not far. Was it a small boat?"

"Yes."

"I'm sure they pulled in somewhere or came back early."

"I'm sure."

Elena was very cold in her light sweater, and the sky was overcast and quite dark. She needed to go back home before going to the marina to check on Nikolas.

Her dreams were back in her mind, and she could not quite understand the meaning yet. Elena wanted to be comfortable when she joined Nikolas and Codros.

She quickly walked from the dig to her apartment building to put a raincoat, heavier sweater and a hat on.

While in her bedroom, the rustling of the drapes brought her attention to the windows that had been left open. Not wanting a wet floor again, she quickly closed them.

Elena's view of the window and the drapes brought the images of her dreams flashing through her mind.

Her dreams were connecting and becoming a clearer picture of what had happened to another couple so many years ago.

The result created the visualization of a man dying and a woman lessening her sense of loss by painting a picture of her lover coming home by sea.

She knew the man had been killed, which quickly focused her fear on Nikolas out sailing in extremely bad weather.

Panic was setting in as she left her apartment and ran toward Chersonesus and its harbor. Elena was convincing herself that Nikolas' life was in danger.

Her mind began to imagine his small boat sinking in the bad weather and he and Codros drowning in the violent seas.

"*My dreams have been a warning*" was the overpowering thought repeating in her head. Elena's quick pace turned back into a run as she cleared the hotel grounds and paralleled the cliffs on her way to Chersonesus.

Both Codros and Nikolas were calm and went about their responsibilities when the wind speed was about 15 knots. They sailed on a reach away from shore for quite some time to put as much stress on the boat as they could. When they turned to head back to Chersonesus, it seemed that the velocity of the wind had increased dramatically.

They talked about what they needed to do before they made their turn toward Chersonesus, but Nikolas saw the apprehension in Codros' face as they talked. Nikolas was feeling a little trepidation himself. Large swells might be uncomfortable, but large breaking swells were quite dangerous.

They put on their foul-weather gear and life preservers just before turning. Nikolas was carefully steering the small boat in the least destructive direction as they tried to make their way closer to the harbor entrance. He was taking his bearings each time they would come to the top of a swell and adjust his course while Codros re-trimmed sails. In a loud voice Nikolas asked,

"How are you holding up?"

Codros looked over his shoulder.

Nikolas could see the result of the last few hours of fighting the weather.

"I am a little tired, but I'll be fine. How much longer before we're in the harbor?"

"Maybe thirty more minutes. Would you like to trade positions with me? It would be less physical."

"I'll keep trimming. If the boat sinks, I can blame you." Codros had to force a smile, and Nikolas saw the concern in his eyes.

Nikolas was having a hard time keeping the boat from trying to turn into the wind as they went down the swells.

Elena was still running when she passed St. Vladimir Cathedral on her way to the harbor. She was emotionally out of control and couldn't keep the thought of Nikolas dying in a tragic sailing accident out of her mind.

She slowed her pace as she started down the hill behind the Cathedral.

When the stern of the boat lifted out of the water as they crested a swell, Nikolas lost steering, and the bow began to round into the wind placing the boat broadside to the cresting swell.

Codros was not quick enough at releasing the sails, and the small boat broached and was laid on her side with the sails slightly submerged in the Black Sea.

When Elena got to the dock, no one was in sight.

Without reason she walked to the end and looked for Nikolas.

A small boat was tied securely, but it looked like it had been tied to the dock for a long time.

Her fear of what might have happened to Nikolas raised another level as she knew they had not returned.

Codros had been thrown out of the cockpit and landed on top of the sail that was now lying on top of the water. The cockpit had filled with water. Nikolas threw Codros the loose end of the main sheet, and Codros tied it around his upper body just under his arms. Nikolas dragged him back to the boat just as the boat started to rise on the next swell. When she came upright, Nikolas could steer once again, and Codros re-trimmed sails with a little more respect for his responsibility.

Nikolas put the boat on the safest point of sail to give him time to reevaluate their position and the weather.

"I don't want to do that again," came from Codros.

"We were lucky we didn't lose the rigging. I don't think we can make the entrance to Chersonesus without repeating the broach. I'm going to run us off down the coast and then tack back."

"I'm wet, cold and tired," came back from Codros.

"We are not going to be back soon. After the next swell check below for some dry cloths."

Codros came back on deck right away.

"Nothing. We're in some trouble here, aren't we?"

Elena was staring blankly toward the outcropping of land that protected the dock from the open waters of the harbor when she heard a man who spoke Russian.

"Are you waiting for Codros and the American?"

She turned to see a well-dressed man in a raincoat, standing back from her.

"Yes, I am. Have you heard from them?"

He saw the fear in her eyes.

"No, but I'm sure they will be fine. Do they have a cell phone?"

Elena hated to be patronized.

"They both do, but I'm sure they don't work well underwater."

"I didn't mean…"

"I'm sure you didn't."

"You can see the harbor entrance from the top of the hill. Will you join me? Perhaps we can see them returning?"

Elena was happy for the company and walked back down the dock and toward the top of the hill west of the Cathedral. Her mind was once again going to the dark side.

Nikolas was worried about the possible effect of hypothermia. They had a long way to go before turning to come back. Nikolas was dry under his foul-weather gear. Looking at Codros, he could see the first signs of fear, and they couldn't survive if either one of them panicked.

"I want you to come take the tiller for a few minutes."

Codros expression was puzzled.

"I'm going to go below and take off my sweater and find something for you to dry off your upper body. Then put the sweater on, dry the inside of the foul-weather gear and put it back on."

"You'll get cold. We are better off with only one of us cold."

Nikolas had no time for arguments.

"Do what I ask. I believe you'll be suffering from the effects of hypothermia in a very short time. That won't help us at all, will it?"

Codros wasn't thinking clearly already. When they slid over the top of the next swell, Codros took over the tiller, and Nikolas went below, removed his sweater and found some rather dirty but dry rags for Codros to dry himself. They changed positions, and Nikolas reevaluated their current capability and the risks they were facing.

Codros reappeared from below and looked a little better. Nikolas wanted to tell Codros what he thought the best option was.

"Each swell, we slide over, takes us closer to shore. I have never sailed here, but from the shore I've seen people standing a long way out on submerged rocks. I don't care how strong this boat is; it won't like a rock if we hit one. If we increase our angle on the swells, we run the risk of broaching the boat again, and we know we don't like that."

Codros didn't smile; he just stayed fixed on Nikolas.

"We need to turn the boat, and, I believe, we'll enter Sevastopol harbor on a safer point of sail. What do you think?"

Codros saw no signs of panic in the face he was focused on, but the stress of their situation had removed all expression from Nikolas' eyes.

"We need to get in someplace before our luck runs out. I have not seen any sign of this wind subsiding any time soon, and that was the first time I have been propelled into the water. If we can avoid another knockdown and live through the night, I will be very happy."

Elena got tired of standing on the hill looking out at the dark harbor entrance. She returned to the dock again, waiting for the small boat to come into sight. The gentleman, that had kept her company, had gone to report the small boat as overdue to the harbor authorities in Sevastopol who also covered Chersonesus. Elena's eyes filled with tears once again.

She couldn't rid herself of the image of the young woman painting a scene of a small ship that would never sail back into the harbor for her. She had never felt the man, she waited for and dreamed of, with his arms wrapped around her or him making love to her.

Elena felt she would die if the same thing happened to her.

"Elena."

She turned to see Nikolas standing behind her.

Codros stood back and watched Elena literally jump on Nikolas almost knocking him to the dock. They kissed and hugged as if he had survived a war. He heard Elena first.

"I was so scared." She kissed him again before she continued.

"I had dreams the last few nights. I'll tell you later."

"It wasn't my best day of sailing." Codros started to laugh, and Elena gave Codros a hug hello and returned her attention to Nikolas. He pulled off his foul-weather gear as he explained to Elena what had happened. Codros took the gear from Nikolas and suggested all three of them return to the hotel, find a table and order something warm to drink and a little to eat. Elena kissed Codros on the cheek, saying, "Thank you for watching over him."

"I think it was the other way around."

She thanked the marketing director, who had reappeared, and Nikolas shook his hand and told him how lucky he felt being in such bad weather with such a great boat.

Nikolas and Elena walked back to the hotel, sharing stories of dreams and the adventurous day of sailing while Codros received a ride back allowing him to change into dry clothing before he rejoined them.

When the three met in the lobby, they looked a little weathered from the day's experience. After Codros settled in and had two brandies, he changed the subject to his new racing yacht.

"I wanted to discuss a shipyard in Balaklava on the sail today, but we were preempted. Tonight may not be the best time, but Nikolas goes back tomorrow."

"Nikolas and I were in Balaklava on Sunday. I could not show him the boatyard because it began to rain."

"Perhaps next time Nikolas comes you can take him back again."

Elena continued, "We could go later this week."

Codros looked at Nikolas, waiting for his response.

"I decided to stay for another week. I have all my work on the computer, and I'd like to spend a little more time with the metal people. Tell me about the shipyard."

Codros just smiled.

"Perhaps we should finish this discussion in the morning?"

Nikolas and Elena said, "No" in unison, and Codros continued.

"There is a shipyard in Balaklava, capable of constructing your design. I would like you to visit the yard and advise me regarding your thoughts about their capability." Codros was watching Elena become quite excited about the thought of Nikolas spending time in Sevastopol, building a boat. Codros thought to himself that she was as much in love with Nikolas as he was with her.

Nikolas commented, "I have several simulation programs I want to run with the information we've received today. And I want to review the results of the J24 comparisons."

While Nikolas was talking to Codros, the server placed the appetizers on their table.

"I could go to the shipyard day after tomorrow."

"I'll call the owner and check his schedule and let you know what time will work for him. I don't want you to accept this new material or the shipyard because I favor them."

Nikolas looked at Elena and then to Codros before he answered.

"You have a reputation of achieving your goals, including yacht racing. I have a reputation of designing and building winning boats. I won't allow either one of us to make an emotional decision about our project. You'll win the Cape Town to Rio race."

"I've come to expect that kind of answer from you. I need to call home and see if I'm still married and tell them about our day. It's time for me to say good-bye to you both. Please, sign the tab for me when you're done." Codros stood and hugged Elena first. As he gently held her, he whispered,

"I do not pretend to understand fate, I try only to recognize it. You are both wonderful people that belong together. I think we all learned that today. Good luck to you."

"Thank you so much for bringing him to me."

Codros acknowledged with a smile and hugged Nikolas next.

"Athens isn't far away; I would like you and Elena to come and meet my family before you return to California."

"We'll call in a few days and work out a schedule. It would be our pleasure. Thank you for all you've done for us."

"I believe your fate was sealed several millennia ago. Just enjoy what life gives both of you."

Elena gave Codros a kiss on the cheek, and Nikolas shook his hand, thanking him one more time. The young couple stood for a moment watching Codros walk toward the elevator lobby. They sat again, ate a little more and finished their wine in silence, looking at one another until Elena said, "I'm a little chilly. Are you ready to go?"

"Yes."

Nikolas signed for Codros, and they walked to their flat. Nikolas took off his shoes and stripped down to his shorts and a t-shirt, picked up his laptop and sat down on the bed. Elena had taken her sweater off and asked Nikolas, "Checking your e-mail?"

"Yes, everyone is waking up in California, and I need to rearrange my schedule for the week."

"I'll get ready for bed first."

Nikolas looked up from his computer.

"Can I have a kiss first?"

Elena smiled and crawled across the bed and gave him a long kiss before she disappeared into the bathroom. Nikolas logged into his e-mail and saw one from his mother. He decided to respond to the others before he read hers. Several dealt with scheduling tank and computer time, which he rearranged to fit what he felt would be his new schedule.

He had just opened his mother's e-mail when Elena came out of the bathroom with a towel wrapped around her. She crossed her side of the bed again and sat next to Nikolas.

"Any from an old girlfriend I can read?"

"No, but I got a response from my Mom to the one I sent to her and Dad, telling them about you."

"Should I leave you alone for a moment?"

"No, stay here. I'll show you what I wrote to them, and then we can read her response."

Nikolas opened his sent file, found the e-mail he had sent, and opened it for Elena. She read it and looked at Nikolas.

"It is very sweet and exactly how I feel as well. Are you sure you do not want to read her response first?"

"You don't know her, but she always looks at things in a positive light. It's OK." Nikolas went back to his in-box and opened the e-mail.

"My dearest son,

Your father and I have read your e-mail many times and talked about how we felt and how happy we were for you. First of all, say hello to Elena for both of us, and we cannot wait to meet this wonderful young lady in person. Your father and I feel you should stay in Sevastopol a little longer if you have not already decided to do so. We also had quite a few discussions about sharing part of your childhood with you. Both of us finally agreed: it was time to communicate what we saw and heard when you were quite young.

Before you were in kindergarten, we'd hear you talking in your sleep. When we entered your room you would be lying on your back, quite active physically, but most importantly you would be talking in a foreign language. The first time I heard you, I thought it could have been Spanish because of your babysitter, but your father said no. He told me you were speaking Greek in your sleep. When your dad was out of town, I recorded one of your sessions and took the tape to an interpreter. Although she couldn't understand most of it, as you were a child, she confirmed you were speaking Greek. The following is from the book "The Prophet", written by Kahlil Gibran, and both of us feel the quotation is applicable.

"It was but yesterday we met in a dream.

You have sung to me in my aloneness, and I of your longings have built a tower in the sky...

If in the twilight of memory we should meet once more, we shall speak again together and you shall sing to me a deeper song.

And if our hands should meet in another dream, we shall build another tower in the sky."

*Your father and I both believe you have found your
home once more as well as your true love.
Congratulations to you both.*

*Elena, you are most welcome in our family and
thank you for finding our son out of all the men in the
world, thank you for waiting.*

*We love you both and look forward to hearing from
you soon.*

Mom and Dad"

Nikolas' tears were falling on his keyboard, causing
him to wipe his eyes.

Elena kissed his cheek with tears falling from her
eyes.

"Is your mother like this all the time?"

"She has always been spiritual in her view of life,
and yes, I've gotten other letters that have touched my
heart, but nothing like this."

Nikolas wiped Elena's tears from her cheeks.

"I'm going to shower, and get ready for bed."

"Can I write back to her?"

"Please, she would love to hear from you. Say hello
to my father as well. He's not Internet friendly, but he'll
read your e-mail."

Elena took the computer from Nikolas, and he
headed into the bathroom for a good hot thoughtful
shower. She finished a short thank-you note and
expressed how grateful she was for Nikolas coming into
her life.

Elena stopped short of telling them about some of her dreams.

She took his computer back into the living room and brought one large candle back into the bedroom. She sat it on the small table next to the bed, lit it, turned the light off, dropped her towel and got into bed.

With the words from Nikolas' mother and Kahlil Gibran, passing through her mind time and time again, she waited for Nikolas.

When he came out of the steaming bathroom, the bedroom seemed dark until his eyes adjusted.

He could see the back of Elena's head in the candlelight and crossed the room to climb into his side of the bed.

Once under the thin blanket and sheet, he reached for her.

Elena drew Nikolas very close to her, and he realized she was naked.

His hands as well as hers began to explore areas they had respectfully stayed away from before these first few moments of their physical relationship.

Elena helped Nikolas slip out of his clean boxers and then drew him even closer.

They began kissing each other deeply and tenderly as they both felt one another's bodies react to the stimulus.

Nikolas stopped for a moment and pulled his head back so he could see Elena's face in the candlelight.

"I love you. I believe now that I've loved you for a very long time."

"Then make love to me. Make love to me like we have both dreamed about."

Nikolas and Elena spent most of the night discovering each other's bodies and finding joy each time a caress created pleasure.

They didn't remember falling asleep, only waking to the first rays of the sun that gave them the light and the desire to start all over again.

REUNITED

"He felt now that he was not simply close to her, but that he did not know where he ended and she began."

~Leo Tolstoy ~

Elena left Nikolas exhausted and in bed.

She got ready for work quickly and wrote Nikolas a note to say good morning and asked that he meet her after work as she had a lunch appointment.

She left the note and the keys next to the bed and smiled at the beautiful man asleep under her sheets and blankets.

When Nikolas woke about an hour after Elena had gone to work, he was still in a dream world. He got up and found Elena's short note. His thoughts were with her as he got ready for the day and cleaned up the flat. He spent time reviewing his unread e-mails and retrieved his voice mail. Nikolas scheduled a meeting for the next morning with the metal people and, based on Codros' message, called the boatyard and scheduled a walkthrough for the next day as well. Once he checked everything off his morning to do list, he decided to take a walk to the boat dock in Chersonesus. Instead of the boat dock, Nikolas found himself standing in front of St. Vladimir Cathedral. He took a deep breath and stepped in. Nikolas walked around for a while admiring the frescoes and the mosaics, enjoying the peace until he started thinking of the swiftness of his emotional involvement with Elena. He believed his mother was right, and he belonged here. He even believed in the fatalistic side of their relationship. He felt so good and so calm when he was with her. And he finely asked himself, *"What's the problem?"*

"May I help you?"

Nikolas came out of his thoughts to see a young priest standing next to him.

"I'm sorry I was a little lost in thought."

"So was Elena when she came to see me. I'm glad you stopped by."

Nikolas was quite confused, and the priest understood his expression.

"It is such a beautiful day, perhaps we can go outside and talk for a few moments."

"I believe I'd like that."

They walked to a bench quite a ways from the Cathedral. Seated, the priest introduced himself,

"My name is Belen Diodorus."

"I'm...."

"Nikolas Sebastian. I know, Elena and I have been friends for some time. This relationship of yours has taken over her life, and she is struggling with whether it is OK for her to feel as she does. I'm guessing that may be why you came into the Cathedral."

"When did you see her?"

Belen smiled.

"About an hour before you came. I was her lunch appointment."

Nikolas smiled.

"These past few days have been quite surprising and like an emotional elevator speeding to the top of a building." Nikolas paused for a moment.

"I won't share the detail of our conversation, just like I won't share hers."

"You can tell her anything we discuss if she asks you. I'm having a problem figuring out why we are so comfortable together in such a short period. I don't know what I should be doing: slow down, speed up? Do you understand?"

"What does your heart say?"

"Get married tomorrow."

"We could arrange that." Belen was smiling again. Nikolas was all of a sudden overwhelmed with emotion. He turned away from Belen.

"It's OK. Nikolas, the two of you have moved your feelings forward to a place some never find, and you have done this in days. I am talking to you, and I know Elena. She is not prone to making foolish mistakes and has been waiting for someone for years. I believe she is right, and that person is you. Listen to your heart and continue to love Elena as openly thirty years from now as you do today. Enjoy the voyage, my sailor from America or wherever your sole has been. Just enjoy each other every day for the rest of your life."

Belen stood and extended his hand to Nikolas, who also stood and took it into his.

"You are welcome at St. Vladimir any time you need to find peace or a friend. Say hello to Elena for me, and tell her, I think, she can call her mom now."

Nikolas was puzzled by Belen's last statement, until he thought about his own hesitation in sending the e-mail to his parents.

"Thanks for your time. It helped me see my path."

"Good."

The two men went different directions, and Nikolas knew exactly what he would do. He walked to the main gate of Chersonesus to find an English-speaking taxi driver.

Elena's day had gone much better after seeing her friend Belen. Everyone at work said how nice it was to see her smile so broad again. Elena was sure her joy could not get any greater, and the day flew past. As she walked down the center of the lobby, she could see Nikolas standing just outside. She could see a picnic basket in his hand. As she neared, Nikolas set it down so he could wrap his arms around her.

"I love you, only you," he whispered before he released her.

"My sweet Nikolas, how do I find words? "I love you" does not seem to be enough." Elena kissed his cheek and took his free hand as Nikolas picked up the picnic basket, and they walked toward the bluffs. Once settled, Elena opened the basket, pulling out the small ground cloth. She spread out the cheese, the meat and the two halves of the baguette. Nikolas poured some mineral water as she sliced their dinner and opened the condiments. They began enjoying the sun falling lower and lower on the horizon until it extinguished itself in the sea. Conversation centered on the two of them seeing Belen, and what a coincidence it was that Nikolas found his way there not long after Elena.

Packed up and walking home, Nikolas changed the subject. The level of comfort they felt with each other had propelled both of them to this very moment in time and Nikolas needed to express himself before they reached Elena's apartment building.

"As I look back on my life, I cannot think of a time I've actually been in love before. My measure to make this statement is from today, from this moment in time. I love you very deeply, and my life is far richer than it has ever been."

Elena was having the same feelings, but was not sure how to express it. They climbed the three flights of stairs quietly, and Nikolas opened the door. Elena walked into the dark room and switched on the light to see her whole flat filled with flowers. When she turned, Nikolas had another bouquet in his hand, bound by a beautiful ribbon, with a diamond ring at the center of the bow. Elena came to him as Nikolas was about to speak. She placed one finger over his lips before she wrapped her arms around him, kissed him and whispered in his ear,

"I will marry you. I will bear our children and love you and only you through all time. Welcome home, my true love."

Love is patient, love is kind.
It does not envy, it does not boast,
it is not proud.

It is not rude, it is not self-seeking,
it is not easily angered,
it keeps no record of wrongs.

Love does not delight in evil
but rejoices with the truth.

It always protects, always trusts,
always hopes, always perseveres.

Love never fails...

1 Corinthians 13:4-8

www.ingramcontent.com/pod-product-compliance
Lightning Source LLC
Chambersburg PA
CBHW070917130626
46555CB00001B/181